Design for Life

Prior Publications

Other romance stories written by Betty Kleinschmidt include the following books. Each is available online from barnesandnoble.com or amazon.com. Orders may also be placed with Trafford Publishing at trafford.com, by calling 1-888-232-4444 toll-free, or by email to orders@trafford.com.

A CLEAR VIEW OF KANSAS and Selected Short Stories, published by Trafford Publishing, © copyright 2007. A collection of romance stories and how women adapt to situations in which they find themselves: beginning life anew, mystery, and love.

MAGIC ISLAND, published by Trafford Publishing, © copyright 2008. While on business to a Caribbean island, Penny is reacquainted with a previous lover. Can the new found passion in paradise last forever?

Design for Life

Betty Kleinschmidt

Order this book online at www.trafford.com
or email orders@trafford.com

Most Trafford titles are also available at major online book retailers.

Printed in the United States of America.

ISBN: 978-1-4269-3560-2

*Our mission is to efficiently provide the world's finest, most
comprehensive book publishing service, enabling every author to
experience success. To find out how to publish your book, your way, and
have it available worldwide, visit us online at www.trafford.com*

Trafford rev. 7/1/2010

 www.trafford.com

North America & international
toll-free: 1 888 232 4444 (USA & Canada)
phone: 250 383 6864 • fax: 812 355 4082

Dedication

This story is dedicated as a surprise publication to the author, Betty James Kleinschmidt by her children for her 90th birthday. Although this romance novel is a work of fiction created solely by the author, the locations mentioned throughout the story depict areas where Betty has lived or visited during her life. In spite of Betty's personal decision to not self-publish this work herself, it is without a doubt the best representation of her engaging ability as a romance story writer. To this end, *Design for Life* is published to be shared with Betty's friends and relatives, and to encourage anyone who has been told "you're too old" to continue pursuing your dreams. To Betty, this book's for you.

Epigraph

Were you the earth, dear Love, and I the skies,
My love should shine on you like to the sun,
And look upon you with ten thousand eyes
Till heaven wax'd blind, and till the world were
done.

From "177. Love's Omnipresence"
By Joshua Sylvester (1563-1618)
English Poetry I: From Chaucer to Gray.
The Harvard Classics; 1909–14.

Author's Disclaimer

The story you are about to read is a work of fiction. The names of characters, places of business, historic landmarks, and the village of San Isidro were derived from the imagination of the author. Street and highway names and locations in greater Tucson area, southwest Arizona, and parts of New Mexico where the story takes place, are real to promote the authenticity of this tale of fiction.

Acknowledgments

Photography for the book covers, of the author, and pictures throughout the manuscript from southeastern Arizona and New Mexico taken by Dale Brinkman.

Dedication and Author's Disclaimer was written by Dale Brinkman.

Editing and proofing by Caryl and Dale Brinkman.

Front and back cover layouts by Dale Brinkman.

Design for Life

Part 1

When They Were Young …

DESIGN FOR LIFE

CHAPTER 1

A breeze ruffled the feathers of a mockingbird on the bare branch of the oak tree. Emily ran past him, her braids bobbing up and down on her shoulders. He flew away across the narrow dirt road to the fir tree on the corner of the plaza. Emily stopped for a moment, turned, and laughed at the indignant bird whose siesta in the late afternoon sun had been disturbed.

She ran along the adobe wall past the oak tree to the gate, its tall wooden doors leaning against the warm, biscuit-colored bricks. For a moment she leaned against the old wood, soaking up the sun and let its warmth enter through her red sweater, already too small for her.

Emily knew that the Adelita Mountains had been named for Adela, the daughter of Don Sebastian Calderon y Marquez. Adela was a baby when he and his followers arrived here. Shortly after the Conquistadors came in 1692, he had founded the village Rancho de San Isidro, in honor of the patron saint.

The ancient statue of the saint had once hung inside the chapel in the villa where Emily's father now had his office. When the church was built in the village, the statue was moved there and was used once a year as the people carried it at the head of their procession.

She had heard many times how the proud and beautiful Adela had refused to go to Spain and marry a nobleman. Instead, she had married a man named

1

Zarga who had a ranch southeast of San Isidro. The town of Zarga now stood where that ranch had been.

Her father had told her that San Isidro and the land around it had once had five hundred people who were farmers and raised fruit trees. Some apple trees still lived and bore fruit. When the people of the town could no longer be self-sufficient, some had gone to work in the mines. The Adelita Silver Company had begun in 1860 on the north slope of the highest peak. By 1915, the silver was all gone and the mine closed.

At Don Sebastian's death, his oldest son moved the family to a place northwest of San Isidro and started the town of Calderon. Calderon was much larger than San Isidro as by now there were only three hundred people in San Isidro. Calderon was where Emily would go to high school when she was old enough.

Emily ran across the courtyard to the narrow porch that had been protecting the old adobe house from rain, snow, and sun for more generations than Emily could imagine. Up to the double doors Emily ran, clutching in her hand a squashed circle of orange construction paper. "Daddy, Daddy," she called, her shrill cry piercing the silence.

Maria, sitting in the light coming through the doorway, jumped up and dropped the coiled circle she was holding. "Muchacha! Don't yell so," she scolded. "You made me drop the wreath. See?" She leaned over and picked up the coil of twigs.

"That's a wreath?" Emily walked over to the woman who was again sitting in a straight back chair.

"Of course. I've made two already today. I make

them every year. You know that. The day after tomorrow we'll gather wildflowers when you come home from school, and we'll weave them in and out, like this." Her fingers moved around the coiled circle in her lap.

Emily's little hands still clutched the orange paper as she moved closer, leaning against the woman. "And what will we do with them when they are filled with flowers, Maria?"

"You tell me, little one," she said, gently pulling the dark braids dangling near Emily's face. "You tell me."

"We'll take them to the cemetery the day after tomorrow. There's no school that day. It's called — I forget."

"*Día de los Muertos*, Day of the Dead or All Saints' Day."

"Yes, that's right. It comes the day after Halloween. That's tomorrow. We'll put one wreath on your father's grave, one on your mother's grave, and the last one on my mother's grave," Emily said.

"That's right, poor little chick. You're so young to have no mother." But Emily felt no sadness for the loss of the mother she never knew. "My, you're going to have to stop growing Emily," Maria said. "Already that sweater is too small. See how the sleeves are too short? You are so tall for six years."

Emily laughed. "How can I stop growing, Maria?"

Maria laughed and got up, carrying the circle of twigs to the corner where it joined the other two. "What is that you're carrying?" She turned to Emily and took the orange paper circle offered to her.

"Guess what it is." Emily was jumping up and down.

"Stand still child. You'll wear yourself out. It's—it's a pumpkin?"

"It's a jack-o-lantern; only, it isn't finished, see?" Emily said, pointing. "Can you help me, Maria? I want to finish it and give it to daddy. We made jack-o-lanterns in school today and we put them up over the blackboard with our names on the back. I asked the teacher if I could take mine home to give to daddy. She said I couldn't, but that I could make another one to give to him. I had to work on it as fast as I could and that's why it isn't finished."

"Well, we have time then to finish it before he gets home. He had to go over to the Lugo's. Mr. Lugo hurt his back and they had come to get your daddy." Maria moved to a cupboard set in the wall. "There's a piece of black paper here somewhere. You never know when you're going to need black." She lifted her eyes toward the beamed ceiling and crossed herself. "The dear Lord sends so many troubles to test our faith."

Emily also crossed herself and nodded. She didn't know what Maria meant, but she nodded as though she agreed.

"We'll finish the jack-o-lantern while you drink your milk. And there are fresh ginger cookies, too. But only one or you won't want your supper. Now, come."

"Oh, good. You made cookies."

Emily followed Maria through the square room furnished with a couch and an easy chair, several wooden chairs, and a square wooden table near the couch. The small windows on either side of the double doors had no curtains. The fading light of the October day filtered through them and the open door lit the room.

The next room was a combined dining room and kitchen. Like the living room, it opened onto the porch through double doors, one half of which was closed. Emily sat down at the big pine table in the center of the room and Maria put the orange paper pumpkin and the scrap of black paper in front of her. "While you drink your milk and eat your cookie, I'll make some flour paste for you to stick on the eyes, nose and mouth," she said.

The milk was cold and felt good trickling down Emily's throat as she sipped slowly from the gray stoneware mug. The cookie was large and thick and sweet with a strong taste of ginger.

"Here's the paste. Now, I'll get the scissors." Maria set a small dish of paste on the table in front of Emily. Then she sat down beside Emily with a pair of scissors in her hand. She began to cut the black paper, passing the cutouts to Emily. When Emily was finished with the cookie, she pasted the black eyes, nose, and mouth onto the orange paper jack-o-lantern.

"That is beautiful, Emily," Maria said. "We'll put it on the shelf over the fireplace so your father can see it when he comes in. There, doesn't it look nice? Now, run along and change your clothes."

To reach the bedrooms, Emily went out of the kitchen and down the porch, past a small room that had been made into a bathroom. She knew that originally the house had no windows on the street side. But sometime before she was born, small square windows had been cut into the thick outside walls of the two bedrooms that faced the street. One of these was Maria's and the other was used for guests. Emily's bedroom was next to the bathroom and her father's was next to hers. Each had a door opening directly onto the porch.

The door of Emily's room was open and the late afternoon air blowing off the mountains was already growing chill. She loved this room with its narrow wooden bed, a small table beside it, and across the room a tall wooden chest that seemed so high she would never be able to open the top drawer. She measured her growth by the number of drawers she could reach.

Walking across the braided rug, she opened a drawer in the chest and pulled out a worn gray sweatshirt. Now, as she removed the sweater and pulled the sweatshirt over her head, she began to feel good. She liked pretty dresses, silky socks, and crisp, new hair ribbons. But old jeans and old sweatshirts were her favorites.

The noise of an automobile engine in the courtyard filled the room. Emily ran out the door onto the porch. An older pickup truck, showing wear from rough, unpaved country roads, was moving into place under a shed roof. Emily ran off the porch, across the hardened earth of the courtyard, past the well, to the shed.

"Daddy, Daddy," she shouted as she ran to the truck. The door opened and a tall, slender man stepped down, pushing his high, tan felt hat to the back of his head, revealing his dark hair.

"Hello, punkin'. Been home long?"

"A little while. Daddy, come inside. I have a surprise for you, hurry."

"It'll have to wait a few minutes. I want to put my bag in the office." Dr. Edward Bartlett reached into the truck and pulled out a black medical bag, already showing signs of wear. He walked across the courtyard, the bag in his left hand, his right hand on Emily's head as she skipped along beside him.

He pushed open the office door and both of them entered a room not too different in size from the living room. It was sparsely furnished. The walls were whitewashed like all the rooms in the house. The aged beams supporting the roof were of rough hewn cedar. From the office door and the small square windows on either side of it, Emily could look across the courtyard and beyond to the open country behind the Lopez and Acevedo houses.

The doctor's office had once been a chapel. Emily loved to hear the story of how the people of San Isidro worshipped here in this room before the church on the square had been built. She looked across the room to the place where the altar had stood, the marks still in the white wall.

Now the room was furnished with a desk and chair, another chair beside it, an examination table, and an X-ray viewing screen. Three cabinets contained medical instruments and medicines. Emily's father had made this room into his medical office. As Dr. Bartlett put his heavy bag on the desk, he turned to Emily.

"Okay, punkin'. I'm through putting my stuff away. You can show me the surprise." Emily danced beside her father as he closed the office door behind them and walked along the porch to the kitchen.

As he and Emily came through the kitchen door, Maria set a cup of coffee on the table. "Hot coffee, and fresh, too. I'd give you a ginger cookie, but it would spoil your appetite for supper."

"Go ahead and spoil it, Maria. I can't pass up your ginger cookies," Dr. Bartlett smiled as he sat down.

Emily, still dancing around, said, "Daddy, look for your surprise. Go ahead, Daddy. I'll bet you can't find it."

"I'll bet I can," he said, breaking off a piece of cookie and putting it in his mouth. He looked around the room, deliberately passing the paper pumpkin atop the fireplace.

"Can you find it, Daddy?'

"I give up. No, wait. There it is." He got up and walked to the fireplace. "Now, isn't that beautiful? It's a jack-o-lantern, isn't it?"

Emily nodded, her braids bobbing up and down. "I made it in school. It's for you, Daddy. Everybody in first grade made one. I made another one, too, but that's for the party tomorrow. Tomorrow's Halloween and Maria's making wreaths for *Dia de los Muertos*. We're going to fill the wreaths with wildflowers and take them to the cemetery, Daddy. One of them will be for mother."

"Quiet, child," Maria said. "Let your father drink

his coffee."

Ed nodded as Emily spoke, his face growing sad. Emily was so full of excitement for the days ahead that she didn't notice.

Emily had been told many times about how her mother and father had first met. Marian Smythe had met Edward Bartlett, a medical student, at the University of Maryland. Edward had been born and raised in Maryland. Marian had been born in New Mexico and grew up there. On their first date, she had told Ed of the history and beauty of this strange, sometimes forbidding state.

When Ed graduated from medical school, he and Marian married. He completed his internship and residency at a hospital in Kansas City. They then packed their few possessions into a U-Haul trailer and drove to New Mexico. He had planned to start practicing in Calderon, a few miles off the highway between Santa Fe and Taos. But when the news spread through the mountains and valleys that a new doctor was coming, the people of San Isidro met him on his way to Calderon. They offered him a house and office, and enough patients to keep him busy in their little town. They hoped he would consider their offer and come to their village instead.

Ed and Marian Bartlett went to San Isidro and fell in love with the village. Isolated from the rest of the world, in the shadow of the Adelita Mountains, San Isidro had been a community of farms and orchards for about three hundred years. Two years after moving to San Isidro, Ed and Marian were excited to learn they were expecting their first child. Maria, a native of San Isidro, was hired shortly after to help Marian with housekeeping. Sadly, Marian died during childbirth and Maria agreed to move into a spare room so she could help care for the new baby.

Now, as Ed Bartlett pushed away his coffee cup, he moved his chair back from the table and said to Emily, "Want to go with me to get Pepper from the pasture?" Pepper was a tall black and white Pinto that Ed had bought to ride to visit remote patients when the road conditions made the travel by pickup impossible.

"Oh, yes, Daddy." Emily had been kneeling in her chair. She wriggled out of her chair and ran out the door with her father behind her. Through the gate and to the left they went. They walked around the adobe wall which had been extended with wooden planks. Pepper grazed in a small pasture behind the house and grounds. He heard Emily and her father and called to them in a high whinny.

"He's saying it's about time we came after him. He's ready to eat and go to bed," her father said. He slipped a halter over Pepper's head and led him back to the courtyard.

Emily giggled and said, "He's kissing you, Daddy."

Her father led Pepper to a shed and closed him into the stall in the corner. While Ed went out to drive the pickup into its place near the horse's stall, Emily talked to Pepper. She and her father filled a bucket with water from the well and set it near Pepper. Then he brought hay for Pepper's supper.

"There, I guess he's all set for the night," Ed told her

as he put his hand on Emily's dark hair and walked with her back to the house.

When they reached the kitchen, Ed closed the doors and made his way to the table where Maria was setting down big bowls of fragrant beef stew. Emily, in her favorite corner, watched the two people she loved most in the world. A third person she liked was Gary Langford, who was ten years old, and lived with his father on a ranch nearby. She would see Gary whenever he came home to San Isidro. He would be returning to his father's ranch from another week at school in Calderon. His father would pick him up at Emily's house and take him out to the ranch where Gary would spend weekends and holidays.

As Dr. Ed, Maria and Emily sat around the big table, eating the hearty stew, he said, "We'll have snow by the weekend."

"What makes you think that?" Maria asked, breaking off a chunk of her delicious homemade bread.

"Grandfather Lugo says so."

"And is Grandfather Lugo an expert on the weather, too, as with everything else?" Maria said.

"His left elbow has been hurting him for two days now. In all the years I've lived here, I've never known Grandfather Lugo's elbow to be wrong." He wiped his empty bowl with a piece of bread. Maria, muttering as she rose to refill his bowl, shrugged her shoulders.

Emily put down her spoon and rubbed her left elbow and then the right one. "How can he do it? Tell the weather by his elbow?" She turned to her father. "Why doesn't my left elbow hurt? Or my right one?"

Ed and Maria laughed.

"It will in time, little one. Never fear," Maria told her as she brought Ed another bowl of stew.

CHAPTER 2

The Halloween party was a success. The children in the lower grades joined the ones in the upper grades and together they played games and listened to ghost stories the teacher told them. The old two-room schoolhouse was filled with the noise of the children. Afterwards, they had hot chocolate and cookies. When the last cookie had been eaten, the teacher took down the jack-o-lanterns from over the blackboard and gave them to the children.

Emily held her paper pumpkin carefully as she said goodbye to the teacher and left the school with the other children. She ran across the schoolyard, out the gate, past the priest's house that was now vacant, across the plaza, and down the street, slowing at their gate in the outer adobe wall.

When she reached her home, she hurried along the porch and straight into her room. She pulled open a drawer in the tall chest and tucked the precious paper jack-o-lantern inside.

Maria had followed her. "What on earth are you doing?" she asked.

"I'm putting away the jack-o-lantern I made in school. It's for Gary and I want it to be safe."

"*Muchacha,* he won't be here until tomorrow. Nobody is going to harm the jack-o-lantern."

"I know, but I want it to be safe."

"You think too much of that boy. You think he is your whole world, next to your father, but I don't think he really knows you exist."

———————————

Dia de los Muertos dawned sharp and clear. The weather was colder but Emily could see the mountains in the distance as though they were in her back yard. She didn't see any snow.

"When are we going to the cemetery, Maria?" she asked. Emily was seated at the table, eating her oatmeal and drinking a mug of hot chocolate.

"Soon, little one, soon." Maria was already dressed in her good black dress, black shoes, and stockings. Her black scarf and sweater lay over the back of a chair. "I wish you had a black dress, but that one will have to do."

Emily was wearing a brown plaid dress with her brown school shoes and white knee socks. Her hair was pulled back in the usual braids and tied with brown satin ribbons.

After breakfast, she helped Maria clear the table and wash and dry the dishes. She straightened the chairs around the table while Maria swept the room. Pulling on her sweater, she waited for Maria to prepare the doctor's breakfast. As she waited, Emily sat in a chair and picked up Maria's prayer book which was lying on the table. She handled the thin pages gently, turning each one with care as the book was very old. It had belonged to Maria's mother. Emily didn't understand the strange words. Maria said the book was written in Latin, whatever that was.

As soon as the chores were done, Maria tugged on her black sweater, draped her black scarf over her head, and led the way to the corner of the house where the wreaths had lain all night. Still fresh with their orange, purple, and yellow wildflower blooms, Maria draped them over her arm and walked out of the courtyard. Emily followed, carrying Maria's prayer book. At the street, she and Maria turned past the Lopez and Acevedo houses and joined other women and children as they walked down the main street to the cemetery just beyond the church.

"We should have a priest of our own," Emily heard Mrs. Lopez say to Maria.

"But the nearest one is far away in Taos and will not come here until next week," Maria told her. "We'll have to make do by ourselves."

After visiting her mother's grave and those of Maria's mother and father and putting a wreath on each of them, Maria and Emily started back to the house. They stopped several times while Maria visited with friends. This day was for social events as well as decorating the graves.

The day passed slowly for Emily. She returned often to the kitchen to look at the big clock on the wall. When would six o'clock arrive? That was the time Walter Langford and his blond-haired son would arrive. Walter would meet the bus at the crossroads and bring Gary to Emily's house for supper before continuing on across the San Isidro River to the Langford ranch where he and Gary lived.

Finally, six o'clock came.   Emily heard the Langford's truck not long afterward. It drove through the gate and parked near the shed. Emily ran to the door, pulled it open, and hurried through the kitchen doorway onto the porch just as Ed Bartlett came out of his office. Walter and Gary got out of the truck.

Gary was tall for his age. He was almost twice as tall as Emily. She reached up and hugged him.

The older boy pushed at her arms. Embarrassed by her display, he said, "Let me go." Emily's eyes filled with tears. She was learning that it was acceptable to show love for daddy and Maria, but it was not proper to show it for her friend, Gary. Why this was so, the little girl didn't understand.

She walked into the house, trailing behind her father, Mr. Langford and his son. Inside, as the others sat down to eat, she ran out of the room. She came back in a short time with her hands behind her back. She walked over to where Gary sat and placed before him the orange jack-o-lantern.

"Here. This is for you. I made it. It has my name on the back."

"What's this for?"   He pushed it to one side and continued to eat his supper. Emily's face grew sad. She swallowed back the tears welling up in her throat.

"Don't you like it?" she asked Gary.

"I really don't want it, Brat. A homemade jack-o-lantern? That's for little kids."

Emily looked at the jack-o-lantern, lying on the pine table. The tears began to flow. Blinded by them, she groped for the orange paper with the black eyes, nose, and mouth and began to tear it into shreds.

"I hate you, Gary Langford. I hate you, I hate you, and I always will!" She ran from the room, past the arms that Maria held out to her, and past her father who helplessly watched what had happened. As she turned toward her bedroom, she heard Gary saying, "It wasn't my fault. I didn't mean to hurt her feelings."

In the safety of her room, the door partly open, she lay across her bed crying into the patchwork quilt. Finally, the tears subsided and she turned on her back staring at the heavy beams showing dark against the ceiling. Soon, Emily fell asleep. When she awoke, it was quite dark in the room. Someone had closed the door. Emily sat up and put her feet over the edge of the bed. She climbed on a chair and looked out the small window. Grandfather Lugo's left elbow had been right. It was snowing.

CHAPTER 3

May brought spring to San Isidro. The trees were leafing out. The apple trees in the valley had budded and were blooming, promising fruit as the orchards had for hundreds of years. There was an apple tree in the adobe-walled yard of the Lopez house and Emily could see it when she passed through her gate.

The flower beds that Maria carefully tended in the courtyard were beginning to blossom. The hanging pots were prepared and soon Emily's father would put them in place on the hooks set into the wooden beams that supported the porch roof. Emily loved this part of the year. She loved this house most of all when everything around it acknowledged spring.

The mountains were beginning to shed their blankets of snow and the river was growing in size every day. Trucks and cars could still ford the river near the ruins of the old mill, but only with extreme caution.

One day Ed came home and said he was going to the Langford ranch. "I've just gotten word that one of the men was hurt in their cattle drive. Got thrown from his horse and broke an arm. They think one of his legs is broken, too. I just hope there aren't any internal injuries."

Maria put down the dish towel she had been holding. "Do you want to wait for lunch? Or shall I fix you something to take with you?"

"I'll likely eat at the ranch. Emily, do you want to come? You could visit with Doris while I tend to the man that was hurt." Doris Langford, who was Walter's younger sister, had lived with them since Gary's mother died.

This was Saturday and Emily had been wondering what to do with herself. Iris, her best friend from school, had moved to Albuquerque at Christmas time and Emily had nobody to play with now.

"All right, Daddy. I'll put on my boots and get my jacket and hat."

"We'll ride Pepper over to the ranch. I don't like the looks of that river and don't trust fording it in the truck." Emily hurried out of the kitchen and down the hall to her room for her warmer clothing.

Holding tightly to Pepper's mane, Emily sat in front of her father. Her father's arms were around her as he held the reins. The horse moved down the narrow street past the house and continued as the street crossed the irrigation ditch and became a trail leading to the river. The cottonwoods bordering the riverbank were beginning to leaf out.

The day was cool. Emily was glad she had worn a jacket over her sweatshirt. She leaned back against her father. When they reached the shallow part in the river, Ed coaxed the horse into the water. The pinto carefully found his footing, crossing the swiftly moving stream and climbed the sloped bank to the other side.

"Is the river really dangerous, Daddy?" Emily asked as they reached the opposite bank.

"Yes, very dangerous at this time of year. Just before your mother and I came here, a man drowned trying to cross it. It was about this time of year. There was a flash flood due to heavy spring rains in the mountains. A sudden wall of water, coming down from the mountains carried him and his horse downstream so fast nothing could be done. There were people on both sides of the river who saw them, but the water was moving so fast, they couldn't help the man or his horse."

Emily shivered.

"This is beautiful country, Em," her father said, "but it can be treacherous. Don't ever underestimate it."

When they reached the W-Lazy-L ranch, Ed went directly to the bunkhouse after leaving Emily at the house. Doris Langford opened the big front door and walked across the porch to meet her.

"Come inside, Emily." Emily walked up the broad wooden steps. The woman put her arm around Emily and brought her inside.

The Langford's house was very different from hers. There were curtains at the windows. Doris led her to the dining room where there was a big oak table and oak chairs with seats padded and covered with brown leather. There was a big sideboard built into the wall with cabinets above it, filled with china and glassware. In the space between the sideboard and the cabinets was a long mirror. Emily looked at her reflection in it as she passed.

"Lunch is ready. I'll just set out another plate. I made enough so the men can eat when they come back from the bunkhouse." Doris went into the kitchen with Emily following her.

When they sat down at the oak table to eat, Doris

said, "It's too bad Gary couldn't be here." She passed Emily a plate of biscuits. "He had to stay at school this weekend to study for exams." Doris took a bite of the food on her plate. "Gary's balking at preparing for tests now. I tell him to wait until he gets into high school and later college. He'll really know what studying is then."

Emily sat there, eating and listening to Doris. "Gary was just a baby when I came here to take care of him and keep house for Walter. Although he is my nephew, sometimes I feel like Gary is my own child." Emily didn't say anything, but listened and continued eating while Doris rambled on.

It was almost three o'clock when Ed and Walter came in. "I think he'll be all right," Dr. Ed was saying. "Of course, send someone for me if he takes a turn for the worse. As near as I can tell, there aren't any internal injuries. That always concerns me, being such a long distance from a hospital and X-rays. That's the bad part of being a country doctor."

The men hung their hats on the clothes tree in the living room. "Come on in and have something to eat," Walter said.

Doris said, "Yes, come in and sit down. I have sandwiches made and will heat up the coffee. Emily and I were playing the piano while we waited for you guys."

"We'll eat in the kitchen, Doris," Walter said as the two men followed her there.

"Indeed you won't," Doris said. "We may live on a cattle ranch, but the Langford family eats in the dining room like gentlemen!" As Doris served the men, Emily entertained them on the piano with her halting rendition of a melody which Doris had just taught her.

Emily knew that Doris was fond of her dad and they were about the same age. She guessed Doris would like to marry her dad and live in the adobe house. But, Emily didn't want any changes in the house, or in her life with her father and Maria. Although, she did like Doris and her piano very much.

About an hour later, Dr. Bartlett said goodbye and, taking Emily's hand, walked out onto the front porch. "I'll check back on the man the day after tomorrow. Be sure to send word if he needs me. Thank you, Doris. You sure know how to turn plain sandwiches into a wonderful meal. Sorry to put you to all that bother."

"No bother at all, Ed. You know that."

Walter Langford put on his hat. "I'll ride to the river with you. I want to see how high the water has come up the bank."

A short time later, Emily and her father on Pepper, and Walter on his tall black horse, had followed the trail south through the W-Lazy-L toward the river. The south slopes of the Adelita Mountains at their backs were cast in shadows. The afternoon was growing cooler. Emily was glad she could lean back against her father for warmth.

As they neared the river, Emily could see the ruins

of the old mill on the opposite side. Time and nature had weathered the crumbling walls and the mill wheel had long since sunk to the bottom of the river during some long forgotten storm.

"The river's noisy this afternoon," Walter said.

"Yes. I've been hearing it for quite awhile," Ed replied.

"I didn't notice it until just now. It can't be far from the top of the bank," Walter voiced his concern.

Rising San Isidro River near San Isidro, NM

Emily had been hearing it too, but had said nothing. The men had been conversing as they rode along. As they reached the bank, Emily could see the swift current. The usually peaceful mountain stream was higher and had become fearfully noisy. They turned west and rode along the bank for a short distance. When they reached the ford, there was no sign of the easy crossing she and her father had made earlier. The rising water covered the path of large flat stones that lay on the bottom.

"Well, we're going to have to cross," her father said. He urged Pepper down the bank and into the stream. The reluctant horse held back and had to be nudged at every step into the swirling water. Emily was afraid. She could feel the uneasiness in her stomach. Her heart was pounding. She looked down at the muddy water.

By carefully coaxing Pepper, they were carried safely to the other bank, parts of it crumbling beneath the Pinto's hooves as he climbed out. Emily looked down and saw the water had been over her father's feet.

"Pretty deep, isn't it?" Walter hollered from across the narrow river. He dismounted and led his horse to the edge to see over the edge better. Stooping and peering into the water, he yelled, "Do you think it'll go over the banks?"

"Can't say. It might," the doctor called back. At that moment Emily heard the roar. She saw Walter's horse wheel around and race up the trail toward the ranch. As she watched in horror, the earth crumbled beneath Walter's feet as he tumbled into the river. Hoisting Emily from the saddle, her father jumped down from Pepper and leapt into the water. His hat lay at her feet. Pepper bolted up the trail toward San Isidro. Suddenly, she was alone. Emily knelt, grasped her father's hat, and turned, following the disappearing horse. Willing her feet to carry her, Emily wept as she ran, stumbling up the trail toward the village for help.

―――――――――――――

By some miracle nobody could ever explain, Ed Bartlett had survived. He was found later that day in a tangle of trees, caught by a boulder at a turn in the river a mile or so below San Isidro. Walter Langford's body was discovered the next day wedged in the rocks a quarter of a mile beyond.

Besides hypothermia, Doctor Ed suffered a broken arm and a broken ankle. After several days in the Santa Fe hospital, he came home and hobbled about with a crutch. His left arm was held in a sling.

―――――――――――――

Gary came home for his dad's funeral. Walter Langford was buried on the ranch, next to Gary's mother's grave. Joe Ortega's father drove Emily and the doctor to the Langford ranch. When they crossed the river, now a little mountain stream again, Emily closed her eyes until they were on the other side. She felt that she could never face that river again.

During the funeral, Emily stood next to Gary and Doris. She tried to slip her hand into Gary's, but he pushed her hand away and moved a step or two away from her. She stole a glance at him. He turned and looked down at her for a second, anger in his tear-filled eyes, then looked straight ahead again.

After the brief service, everyone gathered back at the

house for the refreshments prepared by neighbors. Ed Bartlett went over to Gary who stood beside the living room window, looking out toward the mountains.

"Gary, I'm so sorry about your dad."

"Sorry?" Gary turned and faced the doctor. "Sorry? Are you? You're alive and he's — he's dead. My father's dead. And you stand here and tell me you're sorry?"

CHAPTER 4

Two years is a long time in the life of a little girl. Emily could hardly believe she was ten. Her birthday had come so quickly. She had stopped growing at such a rapid pace and at ten was just even with the top of the chest in her room. Her father had had to raise the wooden rod in her closet so that her dresses didn't brush the floor, but it still was not near the ceiling. Otherwise, there was little evidence of growing older.

Gary was much nicer to her now. He was thirteen. He had taught her to ride a horse. When she and her father visited the W-Lazy-L, she and Gary would take long rides across the meadows, he on his favorite horse and she on a gentle pony he chose for her. Gary showed little feelings for her other than being kind to her most of the time. He still called her "Brat," but it was an affectionate name now, and she didn't feel the hurt she used to feel.

The day of Emily's tenth birthday was cold and dreary. She wished she hadn't been born in March. Other kids had nice birthdays and could have parties and play outside in the warm sunshine. She walked to the window and looked out, her nose full of the wonderful smell of the birthday cake Maria had taken from the oven. It was cooling now, and when it was completely cool, Maria was going to frost it with yellow frosting.

Yellow was Emily's favorite color. In the kitchen cupboard was a little box of tiny yellow candles. Maria was going to put ten of them on the cake. Emily had wanted Gary to come to her birthday dinner, but he was at boarding school in Calderon and was not coming home that weekend.

Emily looked out at the drizzling rain. There were no signs of its stopping. It had been pouring off and on since early that morning. What was the good of having a birthday on Saturday if it was going to rain all day? Her eyes paused at the sight of the white, yellow, and purple crocuses that looked bedraggled from the rain, dark against the water soaked wood of the shed. When Emily heard her father's truck drive through the open gate, she opened the kitchen door and ran out onto the porch. Maria closed the door behind her. "Hello, Daddy," she shouted. "The cake is done, but has to cool before Maria can frost it."

Dr. Ed Bartlett rolled down the window, "Hello, punkin'. Sorry it had to rain on your birthday." He continued toward the shed, parked the truck under the slanting roof, got out, and ran toward the house, carrying a big black leather bag. "I have to put my bag in the office. I'll be with you in a minute. Better go inside before you catch cold."

"I'll wait for you here." Emily hugged herself to ward off the cold. Soon her father came, walking along the porch, and put an arm around her shoulders. He opened the kitchen door. Maria had just finished icing the cake. A little box of candles lay on the table.

"Hmm, the cake smells good. Looks pretty, too," the doctor said.

"Can you believe she's ten already, Doctor?" Maria

asked, putting the cake on the table.

"Hard to believe. You know, Maria, it was raining the day she was born, just like today."

Soon they sat down to the dinner of chicken and dumplings, Emily's favorite. Emily had two helpings. As Maria began to clear the table, Ed disappeared into his office. Emily got up from the table and sat by the fireplace, eager to make her wish and blow out the candles on her cake. She knew her father had gone to get her birthday gift which he had hidden somewhere.

Maria had already given her a gift, the pretty yellow dress she was wearing. Maria had made it on her portable sewing machine which she kept in her room. Someday Emily would have a portable sewing machine and a straw sewing basket too. She had seen a basket in a catalog and longed to own it. That was going to be her birthday wish when she blew out the candles.

Ed came in, closing the door with his foot as he carried a large package wrapped in brown paper and tied with a string. He put it on the table beside the cake. "All right, punkin'. You can open this before Maria lights the candles."

Emily ran to the table and took the package in her hands. She set it on a chair and began to untie the string. When the paper was stripped away, a cardboard box remained. She opened it and pulled out a rectangular straw sewing basket. She pushed down the two handles and lifted the top. The side sections slid out with the movement of the top revealing the deep interior where one could store all sorts of things. The side sections were filled with needles, pins, buttons, and her own pair of scissors. The inside of the top was covered with red velvet, making a pin cushion. The straw sewing basket she had seen in the catalog sat on the table before her. Emily closed the basket and caressed it lovingly. She raised her eyes to look at Maria and her father. They were watching her. "Do you like it?"

"Oh, Daddy, it's beautiful. It's even more beautiful than the picture in the catalog. Thank you." Emily ran to her father and put her arms around his waist. He knelt before her and gathered her up. Emily could see the tears in his eyes as he smiled at her.

Ed turned to Maria as he released Emily and stood. "Light up the cake, Maria. With so many candles, the whole town will see the blaze."

After Emily blew out the candles, Maria said, "You didn't make a wish."

"I didn't have to," Emily said. "I was going to wish for a sewing basket just like this."

Spring took its own sweet time arriving. It seemed as if the cold, rainy weather would go on forever. The snow had not completely melted in the mountains. Emily could see the peaks of the Adelitas gleaming in the occasional sunshine, their heads covered by white mantillas.

Adelita Mountains north of San Isidro, NM

Sometimes, if the day was warm, it would be a reminder to the people of San Isidro that spring and summer would come eventually. As it had done for centuries, the barren land would bloom again with wildflowers, grasses, and fruit trees. But right now, it seemed only a dream, never to come true.

Emily couldn't play outdoors with her friends in this kind of rainy weather. She contented herself by sewing. For years she had been hoarding bits of fabric, little scraps left over from the neighbor families' sewing. Maria had given her very small pieces as well. Emily stored the scraps of fabric in a big shopping bag in a corner of her closet.

"What are you going to do with them?" Maria asked her. "Make doll dresses?"

"I don't know," she said. "I'm just saving the cloth. I'll know what to do with it when the time comes."

In her mind, she was planning a project, a cloth portrait of the Adelita Mountains. She needed many scraps in shades of blue to make her picture, some bits of tans and browns, yellows and reds too. Her collection of scraps was almost complete. She spent a lot of time arranging the scraps in various ways, never quite satisfied with the results.

Then one day, Emily took out the shopping bag and spread the bits of cloth on the floor of her room. She took down her sewing basket from the table by her bed and lifting out the scissors, and began to cut. Snipping away at the pieces, she arranged them in little piles according to color. She threaded a needle and began to sew, making the first stitches in her portrait of the Adelitas.

Emily worked in her free time all through March, April, and into the first part of May. At last the portrait was finished. One afternoon, when she returned home from school, she took it from her closet and unrolling it, carried it to the kitchen.

Maria was busy, humming to herself as she prepared supper.

"It's finished, Maria," Emily said, spreading the cloth picture on the table. "What do you think?"

A bit lopsided, the edges not quite straight, the collection of cloth scraps lay before them. "Oh, Emily, it looks like the mountains," Maria said. "Emily, you are an artist. Yes, a real artist." She wiped her hands on her apron and leaned over to hug Emily.

Emily nodded. "Yes, that's what I am. An artist." Now she knew what she wanted to do someday. She wanted to create beautiful things.

"We'll have it framed," Maria said. "Maybe Mr. Acevedo, who has a cabinet shop, can make a frame for it. I'll ask him. Let's put the picture over the back of this chair so your father will see it at dinner. He'll be so proud of you."

CHAPTER 5

Gary no longer lived at the W-Lazy-L. After his father's death, Aunt Doris had him continue his schooling in Calderon. By age 14, she felt it best for him to go to a larger high school to provide more opportunities. She took him to Missouri to live near his grandparents in St. Louis. Emily missed him sometimes. The W-Lazy-L ranch was now being managed by the foreman, Joe Ortega.

May dragged on and the last day of school came and went. The Adelita Mountains lost their headdresses of snow. When summer finally arrived, everyone was ready for it.

The Fiesta de San Isidro was a joyous occasion. The people laughed and danced and sang. They ate too much delicious food and drank too much cider. When it was time for the procession around the streets of San Isidro, they took down the ancient statue of the saint, set it on a pallet borne by four men, and paraded it around the streets of San Isidro. The priest came to San Isidro and led the procession, preceded by the altar boys. Emily joined the other people walking behind the saint.

Flowers had begun to bloom along the narrow streets. The fallen adobe houses that dotted the town were softened by splashes of color. The trees on the corners of the plaza in front of the church were fully leafed out. The old oak tree at the corner of Emily's street was a mass of green again. Birds nested in it as they had for decades. This was the time of year that Emily loved best of all.

It was the day after the procession that Dr. Ed came home with the letter. Emily and Maria were sitting on the porch outside the kitchen door peeling potatoes when he drove into the courtyard and parked the pickup near the shed. He got out and walked across the yard, past the well, toward Emily and Maria carrying a letter in his right hand.

"Well, I seem to have a letter from the government. Maybe they want me to visit the President and have dinner at the White House," he laughed.

"Really, Daddy? Honest?"

"Hush, child. He's only joking," Maria said.

Dr. Ed ripped open the envelope and pulled out the single sheet of paper, which he carefully unfolded. He read the letter through, then folded it, and put it back into the envelope without saying anything. He walked to the edge of the porch and stepped down into the courtyard.

"What is it, Maria? What did he mean?" Emily asked.

"Hush, child. I don't know." They sat there, the pans of potatoes in their laps. Ed looked out over the courtyard wall toward the mountains. For a long while he stood there, and then he turned and came back to the porch.

"The letter was a draft notice. It looks like I'll be going to war. I'd hoped they wouldn't need me."

Maria gasped, "You'll be leaving here?" as she started to cry.

"Yes. I'm afraid I will. I'll have to pack up everything and take Emily back to Maryland to live with my sister."

"How soon?"

"A week, two weeks at the most."

"Oh, no." Maria clutched the pan of potatoes to her chest.

"But, Daddy, I don't want to leave. I can't leave San Isidro and Maria and my friends."

All her life, she had known only this historic house, this little village. How could she leave them behind? Being young, Emily could not imagine whether she would ever return. Once she left, would that be it? How would she ever be able to return? She had often thought of Gary. Her eyes filled with tears as she followed her father and Maria into the house.

It took only two weeks to pack their personal belongings and make arrangements to leave. Dr. Ed found a doctor in Calderon to take care of his patients. Maria and Dr. Ed gave the furniture to neighbors. Maria went to live with her brother's family on the outskirts of San Isidro. The house was closed and one key was mailed to Emily's Aunt Phyllis in Maryland. He gave the other key to Joe Ortega, the foreman at the W-Lazy-L. Joe would check on the house every once in a while until Dr. Ed returned to San Isidro.

It was a beautiful day in early July when Emily

climbed into the pickup beside her father. She had already said goodbye to Maria, clinging to her until the last moment. She looked at the empty stall beside the truck. Her father had given Pepper to Joe Ortega.

Her father began to drive the old Ford truck down the drive, beyond the house and the well, passing the flower beds now bursting with color. Maria was standing on the porch near the kitchen door as they passed by her. She waved and called, "Via con Dios, Muchacha. Go with God, my little one." Emily waved at the woman she had known all her life. At the street, Dr. Ed turned and started driving toward the highway. Emily had tucked her knees under her and turned to look out the back window, watching until Maria was out of sight.

They passed the church, the trees now in full leaf. The old houses and tumbled ruins came into view and then disappeared as her father drove down the main street of San Isidro. People stood in their doorways, or came out to the street to wave. The truck turned a bend in the street which now became a narrow two-lane road. Soon San Isidro was lost to view.

Emily stayed on her knees watching out the rear window because she knew there was a place just down the road where there was a hollow and San Isidro could be seen. She watched the Adelita Mountains growing farther and farther away. Then the hollow in the hills came into view and San Isidro, her home, was briefly visible before it vanished again behind a mountain.

Emily turned around in the seat, put her legs out in front of her, and buckled her seat belt. She smoothed the skirts of her cotton dress and looked at the road ahead of her. "What are you thinking?" her father asked.

"Will I ever see it again? Will I, Daddy? Will I ever go back?"

"Only time will tell, sweetheart. For now, we can only look ahead."

"But I do want to go back, Daddy. I will go back to San Isidro someday. I will."

Part 2

The Designer and the Cowboy

Part 2

The Beginning of the End

CHAPTER 6

The metal heron would be perfect under the bathroom window. It had cost a fortune, but the effect would be worth every cent and would add the finishing touch. Sitting in the marble bathtub, Carla stretched her slender body and wriggled her toes as she closed her eyes and thought of how far she had come toward finishing the house. While she mentally listed the things yet to be done, she heard a voice lazily drawl, "Want me to scrub yer back?"

She opened her eyes and turned her head toward the sound of the voice. Jerking her pink cotton skirt down over her legs and tugging at the neckline of her brown tee shirt as she got out of the tub, she looked up at the tall, slender man standing in the doorway and said, "Oh, you startled me. You could have knocked."

"I came in through the bedroom," he said, pointing to the doorway. "I didn't expect to find anyone in here." He looked around the bathroom. "By the way, are you Ms. Carla Meade?"

"Yes, I am. I'm the interior decorator from Design for You. Mr. Langley hired me to decorate this house." Carla looked at him. He had dark brown eyes under thick, dark brows, his mouth now curving up at the corners into a slowly developing grin. A thick mass of gray curly hair was crowning a young face. He was probably thirty-five or -six.

"But you don't look like an interior decorator." He moved closer to the tub.

"What's an interior decorator supposed to look

41

like?"

"Well," he said, his hand on his chin, "tall, skinny with her hair pulled back into a knot. Thick eye glasses. Somehow, you don't look the part." He moved closer. "Instead, you're only this tall." He measured her height with his hand held against his chest. "And you have beautiful hair, the color of the bark of a mesquite tree in summer." He moved closer. "And your eyes are almost black."

Carla moved away from the bathtub and walked two steps toward where her shoes lay. Putting a foot into one, she stumbled toward the man. He tossed his battered brown Stetson to the floor as he reached forward and put his arms out to steady her. Pressed to his faded blue chambray shirt, she could hear the beat of his heart against her face. She breathed deeply, and then pushed away from him.

"I'm all right now," she said, her voice hardly more than a whisper.

"Here. Let me." He knelt before her and picked up her other shoe. "Put your hand on my shoulder to steady yourself." He slipped the shoe onto her foot, his fingers trailing across her ankle and instep. Reaching for his hat, he stood up.

"And now that you've found me, what do you want?" Carla stammered.

His eyes roamed over her. "Oh, you mean what am I doing here?" he said. "Well, I sure didn't come in here expecting to find a lady taking a bath," he grinned.

"I wasn't taking a bath and you know it."

"I do now. But from the doorway it looked like you were. I didn't know what I was going to see when you stood up." The grin pulled up the corners of his mouth. His eyes were twinkling.

"I hope I didn't disappoint you."

"You did, a little," he said.

He was dressed in faded jeans that hugged his hips and waist. His shirt was open at the neck, revealing dark chest hair. Holding his Stetson in his hands, his long fingers turned the wide brim. Carla noticed that his hands didn't go with the rough, faded clothes he was wearing. They were smooth, his finger nails neatly trimmed and buffed. This was not a man who worked outdoors.

"Did Mr. Langley send you? Have you come from the ranch?" Carla asked.

He hesitated for a moment, then said, "Yes, ma'am. He sent me. Uh, from the ranch. He wanted me to give you a message."

"Oh. And what is the message?" She wished he would get on with it but he seemed to be in no hurry. He was a very attractive man. He stirred past memories that she thought were forgotten.

The man continued to look at her as if he were taking notes for future reference. At last he said, "Mr. Langley's going to need this house for tomorrow night. He wants to take possession tomorrow."

Carla looked at him with surprise. "Tomorrow night? But I have to go over everything and be sure that the house is completely furnished and decorated. That takes time. And I have to hire household employees. He's rushing things." She placed her hands on her hips and looked up at him. "You can tell Mr. Jeffrey Langley—no, don't tell him —." She noticed the smile hovering at the corners of the man's mouth.

"This would make a nice setting for his party," he said, looking around the bathroom, then toward the master bedroom beyond the door. "No, seriously. He has a group of people arriving tomorrow from Mexico and the border states—New Mexico, Texas, California, and of course, Arizona. He's going to have a cocktail party here." He said to tell you, he'll need someone to receive guests at the front door, waiters, and someone in charge in the kitchen. A housekeeper or whatever you call her. He said you had offered to staff the house for him. Would you please hire the people by tomorrow and have everything ready for tomorrow night?" He paused, thinking, and then said, "I guess that's all."

"That's quite a bit. Will he be staying here tomorrow night?"

"I think he plans to." He looked down at the hat in his hands. "He'll be alone."

"You seem to know a lot about what Jeffrey Langley wants," Carla said. She noticed how his hands caressed the brim of his hat. She wondered how those hands would feel if he touched her. Oh, for heaven's sake, she thought, what's gotten into you. Better leave such thoughts alone. Uneasiness filled her.

The man was talking. "Yes, ma'am. I guess I do know a lot about Mr. Langley."

"Well, you can go back to the ranch and tell him the house isn't ready yet."

He looked around the bathroom. "It looks ready to me. I came through the front door and looked into the living room. It was all furnished and looked great and the dining room too. The master bedroom looks like a person could undress, get into bed, and have a good night's sleep." He looked at her. Carla turned her head away.

"But you didn't see the kitchen," she said. "You should have come in through the back door and you would have noticed."

"What's wrong with the kitchen?" he said.

"The stove hasn't arrived. I'm told it won't be here for another week. There are a lot of little things that aren't ready."

"I don't see what problem that would cause. Can't you get electric appliances to heat water, make coffee, fry, bake ... that sort of thing?"

Carla continued. "And there isn't time to prepare canapés and other food for a cocktail party. Even if I knew how many people were coming. Even if the kitchen staff were here."

"Oh, I don't think he was planning on the food being fixed here. He's thinking of having it catered by — what name did he say? — the Desert Catering Service? Is there some outfit called that?"

"Yes. And they're very good, too."

"Seems like I heard him say they were supposed to fix the food. If you have the household help in here by tomorrow morning to take care of deliveries, then I'm sure Mr. Langley will be satisfied."

"Well, thanks a lot, Mr. — ?"

"Uh, Jack. Just call me Jack."

"All right, Jack. By the way, as you came down the hall, did you notice a big crate?"

"Yeah."

"Could you bring it in here?"

"Sure."

"It's heavy."

"I can manage."

He turned and left the room. While she was waiting for him to return with the crate, Carla looked around the bathroom. She had been sitting in the huge tub, her arms outstretched along its rim, her fingertips caressing the brown marble.

She was studying the plant filled bay window. Some plants hung from the high ceiling, supported by woven jute straps. Others sat on the tiled floor in large ceramic pots, spilling their greenery and shielding the room from the glaring sunlight coming through the wide panes of glass.

Another touch had been needed to complete the room. That was when Carla remembered the tall metal heron still in its crate in the hall. She had been deciding whether to have the workmen uncrate it and place it where she wanted when Jack had first come in.

Now she moved around the room, wondering what was taking him so long. He must be looking for a workman to help him. She touched the gleaming top of the round table between the two cushioned chairs. She rearranged the magazines on the table top. She opened the doors of the linen cupboard and saw the new towels—brown, beige, coral, and apricot—neatly stacked on the shelves.

From the cupboard she took bars of soap and began to unwrap them. She put them in a basket woven by Indians in Mexico and carried it to the edge of the tub. Taking a bar of soap from the basket, she moved around a curving wall to the shower area and placed the soap on a ledge below the high, narrow window that lit the area.

Carla heard someone moving through the dressing room. She looked out from the shower area. It was Jack, dragging the heavy crate.

"First, you were taking a bath. Now you're taking a shower," he said. Carla laughed. "Where do you want this thing?" he grunted.

"Out here." Carla walked out of the shower area and over to the big window. "Set it down right—here, and uncrate it."

"I found a tool kit next to the crate," he said as he took a large screwdriver out of his pocket. "I grabbed this figuring you would want to open it." He began to open the structure and pulled out a metal bird nearly four feet high.

"I found that in a shop in Sedona," Carla said. "I knew it would come in handy somewhere."

"Where do you want it?" Jack asked.

"Under that window," Carla said, pointing. "Right in the center. There. That's perfect," she said as Jack set the heron in place. He walked back to where she was standing and admired the effect. The tall metal heron seemed to rise from the tiled floor, standing on one long, slender foot, the other foot poised in the air. The metal plates that formed its body glowed in bronze and shiny black in the filtered light of the plant filled window.

"Isn't he magnificent?" Carla asked. "It's from Italy." She went over to the heron and ran her hands over the metal. "Do you think your boss will like him?" She looked up at Jack who stood next to her, his Stetson on the back of his head.

"Oh, I'm sure he will. It's real pretty."

"It's more than pretty. It's beautiful," she said.

"Well, you know what I mean. I don't have the proper words sometimes to describe things. Like you, for instance. I'd say you were pretty, but I would mean you're beautiful."

Carla didn't like the way her body was reacting, as she blushed. She looked at him, her eyes following his slender frame from the top of his gray curls to the toes of his scuffed boots. His faded jeans clung to his hips, the fabric drawn tight.

Do something, Carla, she thought. Break the tension.

"Stay right here by the window," she said. She hurried back to the bathtub, slipped off her shoes and climbed into the tub. She sat down and leaned back.

"Going to take another bath?" he asked, grinning at her.

"Yes," she said. She looked at the heron. "Now, move the bird a little to the right. Just a little. No, not too much. A little to the left now. There. That's perfect."

The man walked over to one of the chairs, tossed his Stetson on the table, and began to pull off a boot.

"What are you doing," Carla asked.

"I can't see what you see unless I'm in the same spot. And I don't want to scratch the boss's new marble tub, so I'm taking off my boots." In his stockings, he stood and crossed the room, climbed over the edge of the tub and sat down next to her, leaning back against the marble, his arm stretched along the rim, behind Carla's head. "What did you want me to look at?" he asked.

"The — the heron," she said. "I wanted you to see how nice he looks — in front of the window." She tried to move away from him. "This is ridiculous."

"Yes," he said. "When I take a bath, I'm usually not wearing all these clothes. How about you? Do you always take a bath with your clothes on?"

"I'm not taking a bath, silly. I'm checking out the heron." She tried to move away from him. "And you can take your arm away."

"Sure. Was I making you nervous?"

"Yes. And you haven't noticed the heron."

He pulled his arm away. "I haven't had time. I've been noticing you," he said. "Well, I've got to go back to the ranch and report to the boss. I'll tell him I've uncrated a heron, tested the bathtub, and checked out the decorator. Busy morning."

"Very funny," she said as he got out of the tub.

"The boss would have kissed you, sitting there beside you in the tub," the man said.

"How could you possibly know that?"

He smiled at her. "I just know." As he sat in the chair, pulling on his boots, he asked, "What will I tell the boss when he asks if everything's ready for his party?"

"Tell him the house will be ready. Except for the stove. And a serving staff will be here. What time will he be receiving his guests tomorrow night?"

He stood and picked up his Stetson. "About six o'clock. I'm sure he'll be here a little before that."

"Thank you," Carla said. "We'll be ready for him."

"And thanks for the bath," he said, turning and laughing as he walked away.

Carla stood there, smiling and shaking her head. She stepped over the side and retrieved her shoes. Carrying them in one hand, she sat down in the chair where Jack had put on his boots. Putting on her shoes, she looked around the bathroom. It was complete now.

Thinking of her own townhouse on East Prince, she could set her entire dining area in this room. Probably the kitchen, too, she smiled. It had seemed enormous when she bought it, after living in studio apartments for several years. But since she had been working on this house, she realized how tiny her townhouse was. The money she had spent decorating her entire townhouse would barely have paid for the furnishing of this bathroom.

No spending limits had been placed on her as far as decorating was concerned. She remembered his instructions when she had agreed to decorate this beautiful house in the foothills of the Catalina Mountains. It was a bad connection and they had had difficulty talking, but she did hear him clearly say, "Go ahead and do what you think best."

For a fleeting moment Carla imagined living here with the cowboy, Jack. She shivered. It disturbed her to find those sensations returning. She had thought, after her break-up with the man who had been her husband for those few years — Peter Meade — that she would never feel this way again. How quickly we forget, she told herself. You're acting foolish again.

I wonder where Peter is now, she thought. I wonder what he is doing...who he's with.

Fantasizing over this cowboy was ridiculous. She had met him only a few minutes ago and knew nothing about him. He may have a wife and ten kids, she told herself. As Carla got up from the chair, she imagined the cowboy striding across this room, his boots leaving tracks from a cow pasture on the thick velvety carpet. She laughed, and then walked through the dressing room. As she passed the brown marble topped vanity with its two recessed sinks, she stopped long enough to check the supply of soaps and towels. She saw her reflection in the mirror over the sinks. She turned away, noticing her image in the mirrored doors that enclosed the row of closets. There was a low chair and a love seat in the dressing room. Both pieces of furniture, upholstered in a rich fabric, were from Mexico.

She walked through the bedroom, a huge rectangular room with a bank of windows rising to a point in the cathedral ceiling. At the end of the windowed wall was a glass door opening onto a high-walled balcony where one could sunbathe and never be noticed by anyone below. Carla glanced toward the mountains and realized the day was growing late. She walked past the large bed, its coral spread and brown, beige, and apricot pillows matching the colors in the bathroom. Passing the sofa and chair with the carved table between them, she went to the door, opened it, and stepped out into the hall. She glanced at her watch—five o'clock.

Walking down the hall past the graceful tiled stairway leading to the bedrooms above, she entered the entrance hall to the living room. The living room had a windowed wall exactly like the one in the master bedroom. Carla looked out and saw her car, alone in the parking area. This meant no one else was in the house, a moment she loved. She could pretend that this huge house, nestled in the foothills of the Santa Catalina Mountains, was hers.

When she had bought her little townhouse on East Prince Road, she had thought no other house could ever mean as much to her. It was her very own. But now this house in the foothills had captured her heart. If she worked a lifetime and saved every penny she earned, she still could never afford to own a house like this.

Carla went down the hall to the dining room, through the butler's pantry, and then into the kitchen. It was complete except for the stove. She retraced her steps to the living room and then went across the hall to the study, complete with desk and chair. This was the room Jeffrey Langley would use as his office.

Well, she thought, as she left the study and went to the front door; everything would be ready tomorrow when Mr. Langley's guests arrived. They would move about in the great living room and dining room, soft lighting revealing the time and effort she had put into the decorating.

As she went through the hand-carved front door and walked along the arched walkway to the parking area, she imagined the distinguished people arriving, greeted by their host. The ladies would be in beautiful dresses, their hair done in the latest fashion. The men would be wearing expensive suits.

She imagined the host, Jeffrey Langley, whom she had never met. He would be tall, stately, his evening clothes tailored for him in Europe. His hair would be freshly barbered. He would smell of expensive, imported cologne. Mr. Langley would extend a perfectly manicured hand to each guest. The guests would remark on the beauty of the house. He would thank them and say that he found it adequate and that it was decorated by Carla Meade of Design for You. If anyone asked, he would reach for one of her business cards on the side table with the name of her business firm printed in large letters.

Carla laughed with satisfaction as she hurried to her 1975 Honda Civic. She opened the driver's side and got in, tucking her large leather handbag between the seats. Putting the ignition key in the switch, she rolled down the window to draw in a breath of the already cool evening air, and started to drive away. Now mid-September, it was still hot during the day, but here in the foothills it was several degrees cooler, even this early in the evening.

Carla drove down Secret Canyon Drive, passing other beautiful houses set on their enormous lots, and turned right at Skyline, heading west. The lights illuminated Tucson on her right. The air conditioning was beginning to circulate cool air through the car. She rolled up the window.

The traffic was not heavy. As she drove, she thought about the newly redecorated house she had left on Secret Canyon Drive. She had had no idea Mr. Langley would want to occupy his house so soon. According to the contract, she had until the end of next week to turn it over to him. If she wanted, she could insist on the contracted time. But the few details yet to be completed could be done without getting in his way. Besides, that cowboy Jack hadn't said if Langley was going to occupy the house beyond tomorrow night on this visit to Tucson.

Who was she to get in the way of the plans of Mr. Jeffrey G. Langley, oil magnate and national cattle baron, anyway? Carla could picture him in her mind — tall, a little overweight, and a big cigar in his mouth.

It was going to be interesting coming face to face with the mysterious Mr. Langley. Up to now he was only a message on her answering machine and one phone call. Carla remembered the first time she had ever heard of Jeffrey Langley. She had been in her office, shuffling fabric swatches. The phone rang. She picked it up. The person talking at the other end was a friend, Saul Watkins.   Saul had been a literature professor at the University of Arizona, but had left to start his "Antiques and Treasures" business across the border, south of Tucson, in Nogales, Sonora, Mexico. Ninety-nine percent of his merchandise was purchased in Mexico and most of it was of Mexican origin.

"Carla," Saul had said, when she picked up her phone, "Can you take on a client?"

"Oh, for you, Saul, yes, I can handle it. I'm just finishing a job."

"Good. This is a big one. Fellow from St. Louis bought a house in the Tucson foothills. Construction has just finished and he wants it completely decorated and furnished down to the last roll of toilet paper. Colors and furnishings are up to you. He can't be bothered and hasn't got the time to mess with it. He'll deposit money in an account and give you the checkbook. Oh, and he wants you to staff the place with a housekeeper and caretaker-gardener."

"Is this guy for real, Saul?" she asked. "What's the catch?"

"That's the best part. There isn't any catch."

"What's his name? Santa Claus?"

Saul's laugh came over the wire. "Name of Jeffrey G. Langley. Tune in on the financial reports. You'll hear them mention him on almost every broadcast. Bachelor—oh, about mid to late thirties, I imagine. Travels a lot and entertains a lot. He's into charity work and on the boards of some restoration stuff. Wait until I tell you how much he's willing to pay you."

"Go ahead."

"Are you sitting down?"

"Yes." Saul named a figure and Carla drew in her breath, and then let it out slowly. "Wow! I can't believe it. Are you sure?"

"I'm sure."

"I could almost retire on that. Why me? There are other interior decorators in the area with a lot more experience than I have." She pulled her chair closer to her desk, hugging the phone between her cheek and shoulder.

"He offered the job to me," Saul said, "but I can't take it. Can't leave the shop. Besides, I'm not an interior decorator. So I thought real fast and your name popped into my head. You're one of my favorite people. Talented, hard worker, dependable ... I told Langley that, too."

"Hey, Saul, you're going to give me a big head. I'm not *that* good."

Saul laughed, "Langley said to call you and break the news. His accountant will get in touch with you about the money and the checking account. You might want to look at the house. It's the last one on North Secret Canyon Drive, still getting finishing touches, landscaping ..." He gave her the address.

"So," Carla said, "he doesn't live here in Tucson?"

"No. He's headquartered in St. Louis. He's out here a lot though. He also owns a ranch at Texas Canyon, near Dragoon. That's east on Interstate 10, as you probably know. What's the name of his ranch? Let me think. Oh, yeah, the Rocking-L. You might

want to have a look at that too. Now, I've got to run –
lots to do. Come see me, Carla. And maybe you can
find a few things for the Langley house. By the way,
how about your own house?   Did you buy the
townhouse you were telling me about?"

"Yes, and I love it. Saul, thanks a million. How can
I ever repay you?"

He laughed. "Wait until you've finished this new
assignment. You may not want to thank me. But you
could buy a few artifacts from me," he laughed. "Just
kidding."

"You're a vulture, Saul Watkins," Carla retorted.
"That's the only reason you got me the job. So you can
sell me a lot of stuff you can't move."

"You're right, darling. How did you ever guess?
Well, kisses and all that sort of thing. I have to run."
The wire went dead and Carla pulled the phone away
from her ear. She looked at it, shaking her head, and
hung up the receiver.

That telephone call from Saul was almost two
months ago. Tomorrow evening the owner would take
possession of the house, complete down to the last roll
of apricot-colored toilet paper. Oh, she forgot—the
kitchen stove wasn't installed yet.

Carla was proud of the work she had done in that
house. It was a house its owner could show off to the
world with confidence. A warm beige structure, it rose
from the desert floor, lifting its uneven roofline to the
towering Catalinas beyond it. It had been decorated
and furnished with all the love and care she had
devoted to her own little townhouse.

Once Carla had imagined living in a perfect house with Peter Meade. She remembered back to when she had been Peter's wife, dreaming of being the mother of his children. But that dream was never to be finished. Carla didn't think about Peter for days at a time, but she thought of him now. Maybe because I'm tired, she said to herself; where was Peter now? She hadn't heard from him in months. An up and coming young executive who had taken the electronics field by storm, he had vanished from her life as though she had only imagined him. Imagined him? No, not quite. The shudders that started in the pit of her stomach and followed along every nerve, shaking her body, belied the idea that he was only a part of her imagination.

He had nearly wrecked her. She had been only a useful object in his careful plans. When that need was over and he was established in his business, he had discarded her like rubbish and had moved on. That was how he had made her feel. Like a piece of furniture no longer needed. She didn't fit into the decorating scheme any longer. Throw her away and get someone new to take her place. Carla didn't doubt she had been replaced. Peter Meade was never meant to be alone.

Carla was nearing the intersection of Skyline and Campbell. She turned left onto Campbell and drove south, went past her office on Ft. Lowell Road, and turned toward Prince. At Prince Road, she turned right and drove the short distance to Saguaro Square. Three speed bumps and she was in front of her townhouse. It was good to be home. She had had a long day. But she still had to call Frank and Alma Ebers.

She sighed as she opened the car door and got out. She felt every one of her thirty-two years. Locking the car, she walked over to the carved wooden door that opened into her living room. The door swung open with a gentle push as she entered.

It was quite a comedown to be in this house after the huge one on Secret Canyon Drive. You could hold a convention in the entrance hall of that house. In this one, there was barely room for two people to pass each other. Carla kicked off her shoes, pushed them aside, and wiggled her toes. She sighed again, in relief, as she went to the corner of the living room she used as an office.

Tossing her handbag on the couch, she sat down at the long mahogany desk and reached for the phone. Searching for the telephone number of Frank and Alma Ebers, she found it, and punched in the numbers, listening as the phone rang. It was answered on the third ring.

"Hello," came a woman's voice on the other end.

"Hello, Alma? This is Carla Meade. Yes. How are you? Good. Say, are you and Frank prepared to start work tomorrow at the Langley place? Yes, Mr. Langley wants you to start tomorrow. He's having a big party tomorrow night. No, it's to be catered. Well, you know how these things go. You never have any advance warning, but I'll help you. Oh, I don't mind. Everything will seem strange at first, but you'll do just fine. Tell Frank not to worry, it'll work out. Do you

know how to get to the house? Be there about nine,
please. No, nine will be early enough. The apartment
you'll live in is ready for you. I checked it out the day
before yesterday. Good. I'll see you about nine.
Goodbye."

She hung up the phone. That was a relief. The
Eberses would be there. One problem solved already.

Carla looked out the bedroom window. Her
townhouse was on a corner. She was able to see the
last rays of the autumn sun peeking through the tall
window. She pulled the shade and turned on the
bedside lamp. She pulled her shirt over her head,
dropping it on the bed. Then she undressed, letting
her clothes fall to the floor at her feet.

Carla stood there and stretched. The air
conditioning felt good on her bare skin. She picked up
her clothes and carried them to the bathroom, which
adjoined the bedroom. After she put her clothes away,
she opened a mirrored door and found a short knitted
robe in wild colors. She slipped it on. It reached only
to her knees. Barefoot and cool in the loose robe, she
went to the living room.

Looking around her, she envisioned the mansion on
Secret Canyon Drive. The dressing room flashed on
her mental screen. She saw the row of mirrored doors
that hid the cavernous closets. The brown marble
topped vanity with its two marble basins would dwarf
her narrow vanity with the fake marble top and two
small basins.

But there was a comfort to be found in this little
house. It was hers. The other house was just a job. She

would move on to another project, but she would always come home to this house.

She would be through with that house on Secret Canyon Drive tomorrow night. "I hope you like it, Mr. Jeffrey G. Langley," she said aloud as she moved across the living room into her narrow kitchen. I wonder if Mr. Langley will take over the house in person, or will he send a representative just before the party begins tomorrow night, she thought, or, maybe the gray-haired cowboy, although I'd sure like to see Mr. Langley. Just to prove to myself that he really exists. So far, he's only been a voice in the distance, like an unseen character in a TV show. Carla grinned as she opened the refrigerator.

CHAPTER 7

The September sun was high over the Catalina Mountains as Carla drove east along Skyline on her way to the house on Secret Canyon Drive. It was going to be a long day spent at the house going over last minute details. She needed to bring her records up to date so that she could present a final statement to Mr. Langley tonight. She had the report in her briefcase.

Carla drove along the almost deserted road, anticipating the day in her mind. It was eight a.m. when she arrived at the house. Alma and Frank Ebers arrived about nine and she helped them settle into their new apartment beside the three-car garage. Then, she and the Eberses carefully checked the house, room by room.

At one o'clock, they were sitting at the table in the center of the kitchen eating sandwiches and drinking iced tea. The telephone rang. The representative from the kitchen equipment company was calling. The stove had arrived and was on a truck to be delivered and installed immediately.

"Oh, dear. What a mess," Carla said. "They couldn't come at a worse time. Why couldn't they have delivered it yesterday?"

"Or why can't they wait until tomorrow?" Alma said.

"We'll manage," Frank said, reaching for another sandwich. "It's better to get it installed and over with. Don't worry." He took a bite from his sandwich.

Carla left the house a little after three, the stove had

been installed, and the workmen had gone.   Now, everything in the house was complete.

When she reached her home, Carla filled the bathtub with warm water, dropped in some fragrant bath oil, and soaked for half an hour. She began to feel like a new person.   She dried herself, applied makeup, combed her hair, and began to dress. Ivory lace bra and matching panties, beige pantyhose, slip and pale bone-colored high-heeled sandals. Then she slipped a white crepe dress over her head. It skimmed her body to the hips, then swirled to just below her knees.

She checked her appearance in the full-length mirror. Bring on Mr. Jeffrey G. Langley, she said to the girl facing her in the mirror. Or, better still, bring on Jack, as she thought of the gray-haired cowboy. I wonder if he would like this dress, she thought. Well, I can't stand here all day dreaming about Jack. "I've got work to do," she said aloud.

She picked up her beaded evening bag and briefcase and went to the front door. It was getting dark. She locked the door behind her and got into her car for the 15 minute drive north.

Mansion on Secret Canyon Drive, Tucson, AZ

When Carla reached the house on Secret Canyon Drive, it was six p.m. She drove around to the garage and parked beside the older model Chevrolet belonging to the Eberses. A van and two station wagons, with the logo of a catering service, were parked nearby. Entering the house through the rear door, she saw the kitchen was in well-managed chaos. Frank, in dark trousers and a white coat, was helping a man in chef's attire. They were arranging thinly sliced roast beef on a silver tray.   Alma, in a dark blue dress with white apron, and two men were loading trays with raw vegetables.

Carla passed through the kitchen into the dining room, dodging the helpers and Alma. She went into the living room, stopped to arrange an ash tray on a polished teak table, and straightened a lamp shade. Her goal was the study across the hall. In the study, she tucked her purse in a drawer of the antique Spanish desk she had purchased from Saul Watkins in Nogales. Carla put her briefcase on top of the desk and opened it. Pulling out the contract and report, she placed them on the desk for Mr. Langley. She then set her closed briefcase on the floor beside the desk.

As Carla left the study, she decided to check the master bedroom to be sure that everything was in place. She turned on the lamps beside the bed and saw they bathed the room in warm light. She went into the dressing room and turned on the light over the vanity. She scanned the bathroom, flipping on a light switch by the door. What a beautiful room. If she could pick only one room in this entire house, she would choose this bathroom.

On her way back to the living room, she smiled to herself, pleased with the job she had done. I am the best interior decorator in Tucson, Carla smugly boasted. But why limit her fame to Tucson. By the time she entered the kitchen she thought to herself, what the heck, I'm undoubtedly the best interior decorator in the whole world!

Alma handed her an apron, bringing her thoughts back to the work that still needed to be done. Alma was placing glasses on a tray and said, "Frank's at the front door receiving guests. People have started to arrive."

"Is Mr. Langley here yet?" Carla asked.

Alma nodded her head. "He came in a little after six. The party's already under way. Didn't you hear the noise? When I stuck my head in the dining room a minute ago, I saw a lot of people."

The waiter hurried into the kitchen.   "Are the

napkins ready? And the extra glasses? They need them in the dining room." He picked up the tray of glasses, grabbed the napkins, and hurried out.

Carla perched on a stool near Alma and helped her fold napkins. "Such a big house. This is the biggest one we've ever managed," Alma said. "It was awfully good of you to get this job for us. I don't think we could have pulled off a deal like this by ourselves."

"Forget it," Carla said, patting Alma's arm. "What are friends for? Ever since we met at the Safeway last year, I've felt that you and Frank were special, like family. When this job came along, I knew it was perfect for you two. No one else could do it better." She got up from the stool. "I'm going to crash the party and see if I can talk to Mr. Langley. I want him to sign the release on the contract before I leave tonight."

Carla went through the swinging doors into the bedlam. The dining room was filled with beautifully dressed men and women helping themselves to the trays of food set out on the gleaming mesquite table. The table was new, made by a Tucson craftsman, but the chairs lining the walls were heavily carved, handmade many years ago in Mexico.

Carla threaded her way through the groups of people gathered at the improvised bar near the living room. The living room too was filled with guests, drinks in their hands. Near the door, his back to her was Jack dressed in a tuxedo.

She would recognize Jack anywhere, even if he wasn't wearing faded blue jeans. She drew in her breath when she saw how his broad shoulders filled out the rich black fabric of his jacket. He had a slender waist and narrow hips. His gray hair was carefully combed and crowned his head in deep waves. His large, tanned hands were at his sides, the fingers curled toward his palms.

He lifted his right hand to shake the hand of the man in front of him. "So glad you could come," he said. His voice came to her like echoes from the canyon where he lived and worked. When he had finished talking to the guests, Carla called, "Jack?" He turned and faced her. At that moment, Frank came in from the foyer and called, "Mr. Langley —."

Carla stared at the gray-haired man as he crossed the room to her side. Mr. Langley? Oh, no. This was Jack. Frank was mistaken. Or was he?

The smile on Carla's lips faded. A burning started in her chest and rose to the roots of her hair until her face felt as though it were on fire. Tightness crept into her muscles. Had she been a fool? This wasn't Jack? No cowboy from Texas Canyon? Was the man standing before her Mr. Jeffrey G. Langley, the oil magnate and cattle baron?

Carla turned and started to move away. "Wait," she heard his deep voice say. "Miss Meade, wait, please." She stopped and slowly turned to face him. He closed the distance between them. "I'm sorry, Miss Meade, honest. I can explain if you'll let me." He reached out his hand and closed it over her arm. She noticed the carefully trimmed nails. She should have known. These hands did not look like they wrestled calves. "It's not all my fault, Miss Meade."

Carla looked at him in disbelief. He was not smiling, but had a twinkle in his eye. "When I saw you in the bathtub yesterday, I couldn't resist saying what I did. I don't often see a fully-clothed woman sitting in a tub. And then, you thought I was a cowboy. The urge to tease you was more than I could stand. I —."

"You let me think you were someone else. You could have told me who you really were." She looked down at the carpet, then back at him. "Jack, huh?" He released his hold on her. She rubbed her arm where his fingers had grasped her. He put out his hand and gently massaged her skin. The corners of his mouth lifted in a smile. Carla looked at him. When he smiled, his face was dazzling. He had beautiful teeth, and his lips were full. He was much younger than she had thought. His hair must be prematurely gray. He laughed, "When I told you my name was Jack, I had remembered there was a time when I was a kid that I insisted on being called Jack. But you wanted to talk to me about something, Miss Meade. What did you want?"

"Nothing important. It can wait."

"No, tell me."

"I wanted you to know that the contract is on the desk in the study. Everything is complete. Would you please sign the release? That is, if you are satisfied with the house."

"I believe the kitchen stove has yet to be installed," he said.

"The stove came in and was installed this afternoon."

"Then, I can sign the release for you now."

"That was all I wanted to tell you. Oh, there is a remaining balance in the checking account; almost five thousand dollars. I put the checkbook with the contract release."

"You may keep the five thousand, Miss Meade. The house looks great. People have been complimenting me all evening on the way it's decorated. And the guests from Mexico have recognized some of the pieces as being Spanish or Mexican designs."

"Yes, there are quite a few of those. You have Saul Watkins, my supplier in Nogales, to thank for them. He imports furniture from Mexico. Only the best. And thank you for the five thousand, you are too generous." Carla turned and said, "You may mail my copy of the signed contract to my office. I need to go back to the kitchen. Enjoy your party."

"Wait!" she heard him call as she returned to the kitchen.

———

It was almost twelve-thirty when Carla looked at her watch. She had finished putting away the glasses in the butler's pantry. The caterers had gathered up their equipment, empty boxes and containers, and had left an hour before. The cars were gone from the parking area. Where Mr. Langley was, Carla didn't know.

"What a first day on the job," Alma said. "I'm ready for bed. If it's going to be like this all the time, I don't know if I can hack it." She wiped a wet sponge around the large stainless steel sink.

Frank was pushing a broom around the shining linoleum floor. "I'm tired, too" he said.

"Put that broom down and go to bed, Frank. You can finish that job in the morning," Alma said, turning toward him with the sponge in her hand. "And, that's an order," she smiled affectionately.

"Yes, Frank," Carla said. "Let us finish with the kitchen." Frank sighed, leaned the broom against the wall, and walked toward the back door.

"I wonder if Mr. Langley's left yet," Alma said a bit later as she pulled off her apron.

Carla said, "I don't know. I'll find out." She went through the pantry and into the now empty dining room. She looked through the window. A late model pickup was all alone in the parking area.

Returning to the kitchen, she said, "There's a pickup parked out there. It must be Mr. Langley's. Why don't you go to bed, Alma. If he's still here in the morning, he'll buzz you on the intercom. I'll lock up when I leave."

Alma was sitting on a stool at the counter. She got up, yawning. "Good idea. Thanks for helping us, Carla. I hope you get paid for it."

Carla moved her hand, waving away the suggestion. "Forget it. I wanted to help you out. Call me soon and let me know how it's going."

Carla locked the back door after Alma left the kitchen. In a few minutes, she would be on her way home. Where were her purse and briefcase? Oh, yes, they were in the study. She moved through the empty rooms, crossed the hall, and stood before the closed study door. She turned the knob and pushed open the door. Jeffrey Langley sat at the desk, turning the pages of the contract spread out on the desk. "Hello," he said without looking up. "Is that you, Miss Meade?"

"Yes, I'm going home now," she said. "I've come to get my purse and briefcase."

"Certainly, come on in," he said, looking up at her for a moment, and then returning to the papers on his desk. She reached for the drawer handle of his desk near his leg. Brushing his thigh, she felt the muscle in his leg move. "Let me help you," he said. Before she could move her hand away, his hand closed over hers, pulling the drawer open. He pulled his hand away and she removed her purse. She got to her feet just as he rose from his chair.

Jeffrey looked down at her. "It was a nice party, wasn't it?"

"I don't really know. I was in the kitchen most of the time."

"Next time, you'll be in the center of the excitement. I'll be sure to invite you. The kitchen is no place for a very beautiful lady." His hand reached out and touched her chin. His fingers trailed across the hair curling on her shoulders. "Yes, very beautiful."

Carla willed herself to pull away and stepped back from him. "I'm going home now. I hope everything was as you expected; the house, I mean. Mr. and Mrs. Ebers have gone to bed, but if you need anything, just buzz them. They'll answer your call. Goodnight, Mr.

Langley." She turned to leave.

"Wait, Miss Meade," he said as she walked away. "Carla, wait. You can't drive home alone at this time of night."

"Why not?" She turned back and looked at him. "I do it all the time."

"Stay here."

"In this house? Alone with you?"

"It's a big house. There's enough room for both of us." He moved toward her. "There are four bedrooms upstairs. Surely one of them will do?"

"No, thank you. I'm going home, Mr. Langley."

"As you wish, Miss Meade. But you would have been quite safe. Until you ask me to, I'll never touch you again. I promise."

"I doubt our paths will cross again, Mr. Langley. Goodnight."

She left the study and went out into the hall. Carla didn't turn her head to look back, he might be standing there. She moved through the empty rooms to the kitchen, opened the back door, and left the house.

Carla got into her car, started the engine, and circled the parking area. As she drove toward the street, she wondered how it would have been to spend the night in a bedroom upstairs in this big house with Jack—no, Jeffrey—sleeping in the master bedroom. How had he managed to get into her private, closed off world? She had tried to keep him out, just as she had kept out all men since Peter left. But this man had invaded her mind and would not leave. Well, she would just refuse to think about him.

The drive home that night with the window open was pleasant. She realized that it was now Saturday. Autumn was definitely here. I'll be glad to get home and go to bed, she thought. I'll sleep late and enjoy what's left of my weekend. On Monday I'll start a new assignment.

It was almost two a.m. when she reached her townhouse. Carla opened her front door and stepped into her tiny foyer, locking the door behind her. She went into her bedroom and pulled off her sandals. She wondered if Jeffrey Langley was asleep in the huge master bedroom in the house on Secret Canyon Drive. "Stop it, Carla," she said in a whisper. "Don't even think about him."

The telephone rang, startling her. Who could be calling at this hour? She went to the bedside table, lifted the phone, and whispered, "Hello."

CHAPTER 8

"Miss Meade?" The voice crossing the wires to find her could only come from one person.

"Mr. Langley?" Carla tried to control the shivers of excitement.

"Yes, it's me. I'm sorry to disturb you. But, I wanted to know if you'd arrived home safely. I should have offered to follow you home. It was so late when you left. I'm glad to hear you're alright. But, I also wanted to tell you that you forgot your briefcase."

"Oh." Carla couldn't remember taking it out of her car when she arrived home. "That's right. I left it in your study by the desk."

"Yes. I took the liberty of putting the contract and your copy of the report inside. I signed the report, by the way. Where do you live? I'll bring it over —"

"Oh, no. I can pick it up later," she interrupted, "in the morning. I'll bring it to you. What's your address?"

"But I can pick it up just as easily."

His deep voice came to her over the wire. "That's not necessary. I'll be going into town tomorrow — or rather, today. I have an all-day conference at the Rio Nuevo Hotel. I'll stop by your place and leave the case."

"Well, all right. What time?"

"Oh, about nine. Is that all right?"

"That's fine." Carla gave him the address and told him how to reach her house. "It's three speed bumps from the corner."

"Three bumps it is. I'll be there," he said. "Sleep well, Miss Meade. You could have stayed here, you know."

"I'll be more comfortable in my own bed, Mr. Langley."

"Oh, I don't know about that." He laughed softly. "Goodnight."

She heard the dial tone and realized he had hung up. Carla pulled the phone away from her ear and studied it for a moment, then put it down on the nightstand.

Carla removed her dress and handling the dress carefully, put it on a hanger. She had paid a lot for it at a small boutique in the foothills. She removed her slip, bra, and sandals. Wriggling out of her panty hose, she looked at herself in the mirrored door of the closet. She looked the same as she had when she was dressing to go to the house on Secret Canyon Drive, and yet, she was not the same. Something had happened to her. She had not wanted it to happen. She had fought against it. But she was falling in love with Mr. Jeffrey Langley.

She sat on the wicker stool and remembered their first encounter in the master bathroom of his house. Maybe I am finally beginning to recover from Peter, she thought, as she went to her bed and slipped between the cool, ivory colored sheets.

Light was streaming under the blinds of the tall window near her bed. Carla opened her eyes, panic gripping her. What time was it? She glanced at the clock on the bedside table; four minutes to nine! She was swinging her legs over the side of the bed when she heard the doorbell.

She hurried to her dressing room, fumbling with the closet door. Finally, it opened and she searched for a robe, finding a short printed caftan. Slipping it over her head, she ran through the bedroom and into the living room. The doorbell sounded again.

Carla rushed to the front door, looked through the peep hole, and saw a tall figure standing there. He was wearing a gray herringbone suit with a pale beige shirt and a maroon and navy necktie. She unlocked the door and pulled it open.

"You're early," she teased.

He looked at his watch. "It's after nine," he smiled. "May I come in?"

"Yes, of course." She stood aside and he entered the crowded little foyer. He was carrying her briefcase. Carla held out her hand to take it, but he continued to hold it as they entered the living room."

"I'll take that," Carla said, reaching for the briefcase. He closed his hand over hers. "I meant that I'd take the briefcase," she said, pulling her hand away.

"Oh, I thought you wanted to hold hands." he grinned. "How about offering me a cup of coffee?" He set her briefcase on the floor next to the sofa and straightened to look at her—from the top of her head to her pink enameled toes.

"Is Good Earth tea all right instead?"

"Uh, yes, that's fine," Jeffrey hesitated. He followed her into the kitchen which was a narrow galley. "Looks like I woke you up," he said.

"I was just awake when you rang the doorbell. But it takes me a few minutes to face the world in the morning."

Jeffrey laughed. "I can understand that. He pretended to write a note on an imaginary piece of paper. "Miss Meade doesn't wake up the minute her eyes pop open in the morning. She requires time to get with it." He smiled at her. "That's an important piece of information."

"How about you?" Carla asked as she took down large mugs from a shelf and set them on the counter. "I suppose you hop out of bed and start your day within five seconds of waking up."

"Not quite. But it depends on what I plan to do when I wake up. Now, if there is a pretty girl —."

"Spare me," Carla said, placing a tea bag into each of the mugs. "I get the picture." Jeffrey grinned at her. She checked the old fashioned tea kettle for water, turned on the stove, and leaned against the counter opposite him.

He looked around the kitchen, then turned his head and looked into the dining area. "Nice little place you have here. Do you own it?"

"Oh, yes. Well, me and the bank. I love this place. It's close to my office, which you passed on Ft. Lowell Road on your way here." She filled the mugs with boiling water.

"I know the address. I saw it on your letterhead, 'Design for You'." He took the mug she offered him. "Thanks." He blew on the steaming tea, and then sipped. "And how's business?" he asked.

"Not bad." She took up her mug and sipped. "I'll start a new job on Monday. It's an exciting project. It won't compare with your house, but it'll be interesting."

He looked at her, studying her face, her figure. "Do you like what you see?" Carla asked.

"Definitely. A little untidy, hair not combed, no makeup, but you'll definitely do." He grinned.

Carla laughed. She couldn't stay annoyed with him. She grinned back. "Do you want a Danish?" she asked. "I have a box of nice ones in the freezer. I can heat them in the microwave. I get them from a wonderful bakery you would have passed on Fort Lowell on your way here."

"No, thanks. But, please give me a rain check on that." He sipped his coffee. "I'm on my way to attend a breakfast meeting. How about dinner tonight?" He paused a moment, then said, "I'm sorry. I forgot there's a banquet tonight. A business thing."

Carla went to the freezer, took a Danish for herself out of a package, closed the freezer, and put the roll in the microwave. "That's all right. I couldn't go to dinner with you tonight anyway."

"Have a date?"

"Yes." Let him think that, she told herself. Actually, she was going to have dinner with Marge Jenkins who lived next door, and two girls who made up their bridge foursome.

"We'll make it another time then," Jeffrey said. "I have this cattlemen's convention going on right now. I'm president of the damn thing and can't very well afford to miss any of the meetings. It'll be over after tomorrow night. Then everyone goes home to his own state, or country. Some of them are here from Mexico and Canada. And, I'll go back to the ranch for a while too."

"Meanwhile, back at the ranch —," Carla said as she took her Danish out of the microwave.

"Something like that, but not for long. I'll be off to St. Louis again soon." He sniffed the air. "Hey, that smells good. May I have a bite of it?" Carla broke off a piece and held it out to him. She expected him to reach his hand out for it. Instead, he leaned forward, took the bite in his mouth, and nibbled the ends of her fingers. She squirmed.

Oblivious apparently to what he had started, Jeffrey said, "Mmm that was good."

Carla looked up at him and said, "Are you in Arizona much?"

"About nine months of the year. Its better weather here than in Missouri,"

She laughed. "So they tell me."

He looked at her over the rim of his mug. "Where are you from?"

"A small town nestled in the mountains of Western Maryland. Oakland. It's a beautiful area. Do you want the story of my life? All thirty-two years in detail?"

"Not right now. Unfortunately, I don't have the

time." He looked at his watch and smiled. "Gotta run, but I'd like to hear all the details the next time I see you." He came over to her. She tensed and set her cup down on the counter. "What makes you go all stiff and rigid every time I get near you? There must be a reason," Jeffrey frowned.

Carla met his dark, glowing eyes with her own.

"Thirty-two, eh? You look like you're about twelve right now. Go back to bed, sleepyhead. Sorry I disturbed you."

"I'm up for the day now. You didn't disturb me, I was expecting you, remember?"

"You'll be hearing from me soon," he said as she followed him to the front door. He opened the door, went out, and closed the door behind him. Carla heard the car when he drove away.

Shivering, she suddenly felt lonely. He could do this to her. His coming into her life was filling the empty spaces. Even though she had tried to keep a safe distance between them, he was becoming important to her. She sighed. He made her feel alive. He stirred the feelings in her that she had thought would never return.

The day went quickly. After showering and dressing in faded jeans and a striped tee shirt, Carla went to the nearby shopping center and bought groceries. The large supermarket was crowded with Saturday shoppers. She filled a cart with fresh vegetables and fruits, cheese, bread, rolls and cereal. She got a cut-up chicken and two lamb chops. As she passed the flower and plant department on her way to a check-out counter, she added a bunch of golden chrysanthemums to her cart.

On her way home, Carla passed by El Hombre, an outdoor fast food place, noting that it was nearly time for lunch. She decided a taco would be nice after taking her groceries home.

When she reached her townhouse, Carla took the groceries from the car and carried them into the kitchen. She unloaded the bags and put her groceries away. Then she opened a cupboard and took out a china milk pitcher that had belonged to her grandmother. She filled it with cold water, and unwrapping the plastic around the mums, arranged them in the pitcher. She carried the flowers into the living room and set them on a table near the sofa. After viewing her handiwork, Carla grabbed her purse and headed out the door for lunch.

El Hombre was a walkup Mexican diner temporarily located next to a vacant lot at the corner of a busy commercial center. Ten or twelve tables with chairs filled an open-air pavilion having a paved floor and a tin roof. Near the street was a small trailer housing the kitchen with a light-weight truck parked close by. As Carla pulled into the area, she saw Tony Jimenez, the proprietor and cook, at the back of the lot. He turned, saw her park her car and sprinted toward the kitchen. Carla laughed as she got out of her car and walked over to the kitchen. "Hey, Tony. You're sure lively this morning," she said.

"I heard your car, and then recognized it. How are you this morning, Miss Meade?"

"Great. How's business?"

"Could be better, but I'm doing okay. Saturday is usually a pretty good day." Tony was in his early twenties, of medium height, with dark eyes and black curly hair. He was wearing jeans and a black shirt. He grabbed a white jacket and put it on. "Ready for lunch? What can I get you?"

"I'll have a taco and a medium Coke." She wandered over to the dining pavilion and sat at the first table.

Shortly, Tony brought her taco and drink to her. He set it on the table in front of her, pulled out a chair on the other side of the table, and sat down. They talked as Carla ate. She was finishing her soda when Tony stood up. "Got another customer!" and he hurried away.

When Carla had finished her Coke, she left the pavilion and passed the trailer-kitchen, waving to Tony as she went to her car. There were now two other cars in the parking area. If this kept up, Tony was going to have a busy day.

Before going home, Carla went to her office on Ft. Lowell Road. She hadn't been in the office for three days, but she kept up with messages left on her answering machine. She couldn't afford a secretary, but she did hire a temp when necessary. When she reached Design for You, she turned into the parking lot and parked the Honda. As she got out of the car and locked it, she looked up at the sign and smiled. The office was small; just one room with a storage closet and bathroom. A window looked out on the street. Several high-end furniture stores were located nearby. Since it was a popular business area, the rent was not cheap. She spent half an hour checking her mail and telephone messages. There was nothing that couldn't wait until Monday.

CHAPTER 9

Tonight was bridge night. Since Marge, Pearl, and Anna would be coming, Carla needed to tidy the house. Her friends noticed everything. Although the architecture of her place was contemporary, she had furnished it in "country-style." She had used a mixture of old pieces and a few good reproductions. The cupboard in the living room, taking up nearly an entire wall, had come from an old grocery store in Mexico City. Saul had sold it to her. She used it as storage space for her books, extra china, and other miscellaneous things.

The dining room table was old and made of pine. It had come from her grandmother's place in the mountains of Oakland, Maryland, along with the old-fashioned kitchen chairs that surrounded it. She had brought the table and chairs to Tucson in a U-Haul trailer.

Carla pulled the vacuum cleaner out of the coat closet and cleaned the floors. Then she dusted and wiped down the furniture and lamps. She tried to clean the house once a week. Her girlfriends said she was a neatnik, but she liked a clean house, and it was good exercise.

After cleaning, there was still time to water the many potted plants within the inner courtyard. Plants were Carla's weakness. Gardening, if only in pots, had a soothing effect on her both physically and mentally. When she felt low, spending an hour with her plants always renewed her energy.

That evening, Marge Jenkins was the first one to arrive. She lived next door and was about Carla's age, give-or-take a year. Carla always enjoyed herself when she was with Marge. Her house, which shared a common wall with Carla's, reflected its owner's personality. Marge said it was decorated in "early confusion." She bragged that at least the living room draperies matched.

"Hi," Marge said when Carla opened the door. "I know I'm early, but I was ready and thought I'd give you a hand."

"Thanks, Marge," Carla said, "but I think I've got everything ready."

As Marge settled herself on the sofa, the doorbell sounded again. Carla hurried to the front door and opened it. Pearl and Anna came in. They lived in separate apartments not far from her Saguaro Square townhouse. The four women met once a month in each others' home for bridge. Their brand of bridge was not found in any books on the subject. They enjoyed themselves and bungled their way through a rubber in twice the time it should take.

"Welcome to the September meeting of the Shufflettes," Carla announced when everybody was there. "Dinner tonight is in the courtyard." She led the way through the dining area to the paved, high walled courtyard with a metal patio table and four chairs, two wicker lounges and two easy chairs with small wicker tables. The large table was set with place mats and Marge's best dishes. A fat yellow candle sat next to the pitcher of chrysanthemums.

Marge was wearing a long, gaudy print dress and low-heeled sandals. She towered over Carla and made her feel like a schoolgirl in her pink and white checked cotton dress. Carla, too, was wearing sandals, high heeled with strips of white leather crisscrossing her toes.

"This is our last chance to dine al fresco until spring," Marge told them.

"You talk like it gets cold in Tucson," Pearl said. "You better not let the Chamber of Commerce hear you."

"Yeah," Anna said, "but we'll get days during the rest of the winter when it'll warm enough to be outside, or have you forgotten?" Everyone agreed.

"Anna, how's Billy?" Carla asked.

"Doing great in school and behaving himself, which is a relief to me. He stays out of trouble and makes good grades," Anna said. Billy was Anna's eight year old son.

The women arranged themselves in the chairs and lounges while Carla disappeared into the house, returning several minutes later with a tray. She set the tray down on a low table. She poured wine and handed the glasses around, taking the last one for herself. "I'll sit for a second," she said.

The women began to talk. They discussed their

latest dates and the latest neighborhood news. Pearl asked Carla about her decorating job.

"I finished up on Friday," she said.

"Did you ever meet the owner?" Pearl asked.

"Yes, finally."

"I remember you said he was only a voice on the phone. Then he really does exist?" Marge sipped her drink.

"Very much so. As a matter of fact, he came over this morning. I had left my briefcase at his place and he brought it to me."

"Forgetting your briefcase was a clever move," Anna said. "I'll have to remember that."

"Come on, Anna," Carla said. "I really did leave my briefcase at his house." Her friends laughed,

"What happened when he got here?" Pearl asked.

"I made coffee for him," Carla said.

"How romantic," Anna said.

"I wish you had called me when he came this morning," Marge said. "When he left, I could have peeked out the living room window to see what he looked like."

I suppose you're going to preserve the coffee cup he used," Pearl said.

Marge said, "You can get it bronzed."

Carla laughed. "Hardly, and if you tease me any more you won't get any dinner."

"You're heartless," Anne said. "You meet millionaires all the time. I know it must get to be a bore after a while."

"They say he's fabulously wealthy," Pearl said.

"They all know about him at the bank. He's on a board or something."

"Girls, don't get your hopes up," Carla said. "He hired me to decorate his home and the job is over. I am out of Mr. Langley's life now. Trust me. Now, how about dinner?"

Her friends helped carry the food from the kitchen. "Everything's as low-cal as I could make it. It's straight out of the Weight Watchers' cookbook so eat all you want."

"Bless you, Carla," Pearl said. "I'm two pounds over this week."

"This shouldn't add a single ounce," Carla said.

After dinner, everyone helped clear the table on the patio. The bridge table and chairs were set up in the living-room. The game lasted until ten-thirty. "Hey, we must be getting better. We finished before midnight," Carla said as she and Marge followed Pearl and Anna to the front door. After saying goodnight to them, Carla and Marge sat down on the sofa, their feet tucked up under them.

"Now, tell me all about him." Marge yawned and leaned her head against the back of the sofa.

"Him? Who?"

"Don't play games with me, Carla Meade. You know who. Is he gorgeous? Is he a hunk? When did you first see him?"

"If you're referring to Jeffrey Langley ...."

"I'm referring to Jeffrey G. Langley and you know it!"

Carla grinned. "I first saw him on Thursday, in the

afternoon, in the master bathroom. I was in the tub."

"How original. What were you doing in the tub, for heaven's sake? I hope you weren't taking a bath?"

"I was trying to decide what the bathroom needed to complete the overall picture. I was sitting in the tub looking at the bay window where I had put a lot of plants. I was trying to visualize a great big bronze heron in the center of the window when in walked this cowboy."

"A big bronze cowboy? I thought you said it was Langley."

"Not a bronze cowboy, dummy. The heron was bronze. It was Langley, but I thought he was a cowboy. I made a complete fool of myself."

Marge laughed.

"Don't laugh, Marge. It wasn't funny. He let me think he was a ranch hand and told me his name was Jack. I didn't find out who he really was until last night. I even had him drag a big crate into the bathroom, open it, and pull the bronze heron out." She passed her hand over her face. "It was embarrassing. Then I went to his house last night to help Frank and Alma Ebers. You know, I got them jobs with Mr. Langley."

"I saw you leaving last night. I wondered where you were going," Marge said.

"Langley had a reception for some cattlemen's association last night. Remember?" Carla asked. "I think I told you about it."

"Yes, you did."

"Well, you can't imagine how embarrassing it was

when I came face to face with him and found out he wasn't a ranch hand."

Marge laughed harder. "So the cowboy wasn't a cowboy?"

"You and he'd get along fine, Marge. He thought it was funny, too."

"But he came over to see you this morning? He must not be all bad. Tell me, what's he like?"

"Tall, nice build. Tanned. Has a head of thick gray hair."

Marge leaned toward Carla. "Then he's old?"

"Oh, no, I think prematurely gray. Only about thirty-seven or -eight, I'd guess."

"Do you like him?"

"What does it matter whether or not I like him?"

"But do you?"

"He's all right."

"He's all right, she says." Marge talked to the walls around them.

"The job's finished. I won't see him again. And we won't have any more business dealings."

"Who said anything about business?" Marge smirked.

"He and I don't move in the same social circles, Marge."

"You could move into his orbit. You could think of something. He sounds exciting. And you could use a little excitement in your life. You've been sitting on the sidelines long enough," Marge said as she winked at Carla.

"I move around."

"Oh, sure; bridge with the girls; a concert or movie with the girls; aerobic dancing with the girls. It's time you got a life."

Now Carla was angry. "You can just mind your own business," she said.

"Okay, I will. But I had to get it off my chest. It breaks me up to see you wasting your time."

"But I'm not like you. I can't ...."

"Play the field? Its fun and I get variety that way. When I'm ready to settle down — maybe when I'm forty or forty-five, I'll know what I want. I'll agree that my way of life isn't for everyone. But, if you want to sit alone the rest of your life and sleep alone too, that's your own personal business. I won't stick my nose in again, I promise. Now, are we still friends? Are we going to have lunch tomorrow at the Foothills Mall?"

Carla grinned. She couldn't stay angry at Marge. "Sure, but a swim first at the YMCA. Not too early, I want to sleep in."

"Me, too. Call me when you get up."

"Good night, Carla. Thanks for a beautiful dinner. The game was fun tonight, wasn't it?"

"Yeah. I always enjoy our get-togethers, see you tomorrow." Carla walked to the front door with Marge. She waited until Marge reached the sidewalk and turned toward her own townhouse. Then she locked the front door and went down the hall to her bedroom. She pushed the light switch. The lamps on the bedside tables illuminated the room.

It's much smaller than his bedroom, she thought dreamily. I wonder if he's home now? And is he sleeping alone? The idea that Jeffrey Langley might be sharing a king-size bed in that large room with someone else didn't please her. Although he might be married, he hadn't mentioned a wife. But there could be a steady girlfriend. There must be an article about him somewhere. Someone might have reported if he had a wife and kid too.

Carla undressed and went into the bathroom to wash her face and brush her teeth. Maybe Marge was right, it was time for her to get on with her life. She wanted to blame everything on Peter. It was easier than admitting she wasn't coping with things. It was easier to sit alone night after night and say it was Peter's fault. When she went out with the girls, she saw couples having fun together and she envied them. Well, she would have to move out into the world again.

I wouldn't date just any man, she thought, as she climbed into bed. The kind of man she would date was clearly pictured in her mind. He was tall and lean, clad in tight, faded jeans and a worn cotton shirt. He smelled clean and manly. His name was Jeffrey G. Langley. She drifted off to sleep thinking how wonderful it would be to be cradled in his arms.

CHAPTER 10

It had been two weeks since that Saturday morning when Jeffrey Langley had come to her house to return her briefcase. Carla wondered where he was. She had hoped she would hear from him. She spent a lot of time daydreaming about him and sometimes, even dreamed of him at night. Her days were spent at the office, catching up on paper work and following up on calls that had come in while she was working on the house on Secret Canyon Drive.

One day, while she was working at her desk, she received a call from Saul Watkins, the dealer of antiques from Mexico, South America, and the Caribbean Islands. When the phone rang, Carla picked it up. "Have I got an assignment for you," Saul told her, the excitement in his voice getting through to her.

"Good, I need another job," Carla said.

"They've restored an old adobe house in the district near the Music Hall."

"Oh, in the historic district. I remember seeing something about that on TV."

"Yes. And guess who's been chosen to supply the antiques to furnish it."

"You? Oh, Saul, how wonderful."

"Yes," Saul said. "Big job and lots of money."

"Lucky you. Where do I come in?"

"You've been chosen to decorate the interior. So, you're the lucky one, too," Saul said.

Saul gave Carla the address of the restoration and

she drove over right away. Carla first drove slowly past the house, which now looked new. The grounds had been restored as nearly as possible to their original condition. Driving around the block, she returned and parked at the curb in front of the house. Carla walked up the two stone steps, and entered through the open door.

A man was sitting at a rough pine table in the main room. It was late afternoon and the sun had dipped behind the tallest building in downtown Tucson. The wind coming through the open door testified to the fact that it was early October.

"Do you mind if I close the door?" Carla asked, hugging herself.

"Getting cold? No, go ahead and close it," the man said. Carla walked over to the table. "Sit down. I'm Professor Cantrell," he said. He was sorting through a pile of old books. "It's getting too dark to see properly in here. It will be nice when we reach the point where we can have lights," he said. "The electrical wiring is almost finished."

"I'm going to have to think of a way to cover it up so that it doesn't show. I'm Carla Meade, the decorator."

"I thought so." The professor stood up and shook hands with Carla.

Furniture was stacked along the walls and boxes were piled one on top of the other. There was barely space to move around. "This is the part that's fun," Carla told the professor. "I wade into a mess like this and turn it into something beautiful. Sometimes I think I have the best job in the world. However, this is my first restoration job."

"It could be a turning point in your career," Professor Cantrell said. "If the board likes your work, you could be recommended for other restorations. I've seen such things happen." He reached into his trouser pocket and pulled out two keys on a ring with a tag attached. "These are your keys to the house." He gave them to Carla.

"Thanks," Carla said, putting the keys in her pocket. "I think I'm going to like this. How about you? Do you like this sort of thing?"

"It's what I do. Besides teaching, I stick my nose in dusty tomes and read about places like this that were turned into museums. Then I find someone who wants to start a museum and we're in business."

Carla laughed. "Do you know Saul Watkins?"

"Oh, yes. I took over his job when he left the University to start his antique business in Nogales. Oh, by the way," Professor Cantrell said, "a fellow is coming here tomorrow morning. He's a business tycoon. It seems that he's willing to put some money into this restoration project." He closed the book on the table. "He wants to see first hand what he's getting himself into. I was asked to be here to meet him, but I have an early class. Do you think you could meet with him for me?"

"Sure, I'll do that," Carla said.

"Be here at nine o' clock then."

"I have to go to my office first, but I'll be here on time."

"Good. And treat him like a rare endangered

species.   People with money don't come along every day.   Now, I need to be going, so I'll show you how to close up shop. See you tomorrow after lunch."

The next morning Carla left her house on Prince Road at quarter to eight.   She spent a half hour at her office checking her messages and the stack of letters that had been pushed through the mail slot. Then she drove downtown to the little adobe house destined to become a museum.

The house had been spruced up on the outside to match its neighbors. Inside, the change was still taking place. Luckily, there was a parking place in front of the house. Carla parked and walked over to the stone steps that led to the front door. The house was right next to the sidewalk, so there was no front yard. Its scarred door still wore shreds of blue paint that had covered it for over a hundred years. The deep set windows on either side of the door held the original wavy glass panes.   Somehow, they had miraculously escaped damage through the years. The hipped roof added in the early part of this century had already been removed and the original flat roof had damage that was being repaired. There were signs of progress here and there, but much still needed to be done. Many thousands of dollars would be needed to finish the project.

Carla was glad the committee had found a benefactor with a big wallet. She had no idea who that might be. The important thing was the amount of his check.

She went to the next room, which had been the kitchen, to see what progress had been made there. She heard the front door open. Someone entered the small front room that had been the parlor in other days. "Anyone here?" a man's voice called. Carla froze in her tracks at the sound of that voice, Jeffrey Langley. What was he doing here? She turned and slowly walked through the low, narrow doorway to the front room. There he stood in a new pair of jeans. His shirt, a cotton check, was covered by a lightweight tan jacket. He held the worn brown Stetson that she had seen before. She looked at him, her eyes following his figure from the top of his crisp, gray curls to his scuffed boots.

"Well, we meet again," he said. "You seem to be into a lot of things." He walked toward her across the scarred pine floor. She held her hands stiffly at her sides, clutching the fabric of her tan slacks. It was one thing to dream about Jeffrey Langley, but it was an entirely different matter to face him again. She forced herself to relax, raise her head to meet his gaze, and smile.

"I didn't expect to see you again, especially not here," she said.

"I wasn't expecting to see you, either," he said.

"I just started working here."

"So I see."

"This house is being turned into a museum."

Jeffrey looked around the room. "It sure needs a lot of work, doesn't it?"

She nodded. "And a lot of money. That's why I'm here early today. We're expecting a millionaire to drop in. What are you doing here? I thought you were going back to St. Louis?"

At that moment Professor Cantrell came through the front door. "Good morning. You must be Mr. Langley."

"Yes," Jeffrey said, turning toward the professor.

Carla hurriedly made the introductions, and then said to the professor, "I thought you had a class."

"It was cancelled. But I'll have to get back as soon as possible for the next class. Shall we get down to business, Mr. Langley? No use beating around the bush, is there?"

"None at all. You want money for the restoration and I want to put my money where it will do the most good. Sounds like a fine partnership to me."

So Jeffrey was the tycoon they were waiting for? Carla would have said he wasn't the type who would be interested in restorations, but what did she really know of him? She wondered if he had heard she was with the project and had wanted to donate money so that he would get to see her. Silly girl, she told herself. What would he care where she was working? His relationship with her was finished. What more could there be? The house on Secret Canyon Drive was complete. She was very much surprised that their paths had crossed again.

Carla turned and went into the kitchen. What she needed was a cup of coffee. An urn was sitting on a table in the corner. A tray with sugar, cream, and paper cups was placed next to it. Carla poured three cups of coffee and went back to the front room, carrying them on a small tray.

The two men were seated at the table, talking. Their discussion stopped while she set the coffee on the table. "Sit down," Professor Cantrell said. "You're part of this project, so you might as well hear what we plan to do." Carla pulled out a chair and sat down.

The three of them discussed the project and walked around the house, room by room. They went out into the courtyard and to the deteriorated rooms at the edge of it. These had been the original kitchen and bedrooms. Traces of the old veranda were still visible. It was nearly eleven o'clock when they had finished walking around the old house, looking at the job that lay ahead. Back in the front room, Jeffrey pulled a checkbook from his shirt pocket, scribbled the information on the check, tore it from the book, and pushed it across the table to the professor. Professor Cantrell picked up the payment and put it in his briefcase. He pulled out a receipt book from under a pile of papers on the table, filled out a receipt, and handed it across to Jeffrey, thanking him for his generous donation. Jeffrey examined the receipt carefully, folded it, and put it into his shirt pocket.

"Well, I must be on my way," Professor Cantrell said to Carla and Jeffrey. He shook hands with them, picked up his briefcase and left.

Carla and Jeffrey were alone. For a moment she didn't know what to say. She picked up the coffee cups and put them on the little tray. "I'd better take these out to the kitchen," she said.

Jeffrey followed her. She put the cups in a big trash receptacle and turned to go back to the front room. He put out his hand and touched her arm. "This was a pleasant surprise," he said. "I had no idea you'd be here." He was standing in front of her, with his hands on her shoulders. "It's good to see you again, Carla."

Carla sighed.

"I think you're glad to see me, too, aren't you?" He looked down into her eyes. She looked up at him and nodded. "I thought so," he said.

"But you're supposed to be in St. Louis."

"I've been there and returned to Tucson twice since I saw you last."

"It must cost a fortune in airplane tickets."

"Oh, I have my own plane. I just call the pilot and I'm on my way."

"You didn't contact me when you got back to Tucson."

"Did you want me to call you? I thought about it. Something always got in the way. Besides, I didn't want to interfere in your life." He took one hand from her shoulder and looked at his watch. "It's lunch time," he said. "Could you close up shop and come with me to have something to eat?"

"Of course," she said as he released his hold on her. "There's a good Mexican restaurant nearby, a neighborhood landmark. It's been here for many years, and one of my favorites."

"Then, let's get out of here and go eat." He waited while Carla went to the back of the house to check the rear door. When she returned, they went out the front door, locking it behind them. Carla put the keys in her purse. She and Jeffrey walked toward the restaurant in the next block.

"I suppose this was all residential at one time," he said.

"Yes, it was," Carla said. "This is the heart of old Tucson. They call it the Old Pueblo. Professor Cantrell said Tucson is one of the oldest continuously inhabited areas in America with archeological discoveries dating back to 800 BC. The city of Tucson was founded about 1775, roughly 150 years after the Pilgrims landed in Massachusetts. A lot of those old houses were torn down to build the Community Center and all the modern buildings you see around us. Fortunately, they saved a few of the old ones, only because they weren't in the way of so-called "progress." Little by little, the people who lived in these houses moved somewhere else, although, some descendents of the old timers do still live here. People with enough money to do so, came to this neighborhood and began to restore the houses. Most of them have now been turned into offices and shops. I love the adobe house that's being turned into a museum. I'd even like to live in this area."

Jeffrey said, "The house reminds me of the one I live in at the ranch. Only my house is a little bit larger. It's not built around a courtyard. It has a red tile roof, but the house is adobe like this one. I don't know exactly how old the ranch house is, but it sure isn't new."

"I love old houses," Carla said. "They have

character, like people."

"Maybe we could find you an old adobe in a nice neighborhood. I don't know what your income is, but —."

"Now, don't get any ideas about me buying an old adobe house and moving into it," Carla said. "I could barely afford the townhouse I have now, and you're certainly not going to buy an old adobe for me."

"I wouldn't think of it. I'm not going to start managing your life. I have too many other things to keep me busy. I was only thinking that it's a shame people can't have what they really want."

"How many of us ever have what we really want?" Carla sighed.

"I guess you're right about that, but a little help along the way sure is nice."

They had arrived at the restaurant. It was in an old one-story building of frame construction, sitting on the edge of a small corner lot. A parking area at one side separated it from the house next to it. The buildings obviously had been there a long, long time.

Carla and Jeffrey crossed the arbor that served as a porch. People were sitting at the tables, plates of wonderful smelling food in front of them. Jeffrey pushed open the massive, carved door and he and Carla went inside. The room was filled to capacity with chairs and tables of various sizes.

A middle-aged woman came up to them. "Two for lunch?" she asked.

They followed her to a small table in the center of the room. When they were seated, she handed them menus. They looked around at the other diners. All the tables were occupied. "We got the last table," Carla said. "We're lucky we didn't have to wait. This is a popular place."

"It looks old," Jeffrey said.

"It is. The same couple has owned it for many, many years."

The waitress came over to them. "Ready to order?" she asked.

"Yes," Jeffrey said.

The woman turned to Carla. "Have you decided, ma'am?"

"I'll have the flautas." She turned to Jeffrey. "They're delicious, served with sour cream and guacamole." She turned back to the server. "I'll have coffee and the fresh fruit cup for dessert."

"I'll have the flautas and coffee too," Jeffrey said.

As they waited for their orders to be filled, Jeffrey and Carla looked around the room, taking in the paintings of Tucson and the surrounding mountains, the fiestas, and rodeos. There was a statue of the Virgin Mary in one corner. Bouquets of huge paper flowers filled vases on all the tables.

When the food arrived, Carla and Jeffrey began to eat. They talked very little during their lunch. The server refilled their coffee cups and left. Jeffrey said, "I promised to hear your life's story. Want to tell it now?"

"Not really. As I said, it's boring."

"Then, bore me. I don't have anything else to do."

"All right. Just remember, you asked for it. I think I told you I'm from Western Maryland." Jeffrey nodded.

"It's a beautiful area," Carla said. "All mountains, valleys, rivers, creeks; not at all like Tucson. Even the mountains are different."

Carla looked out the window to where a mountain range framed the blue sky. "I was an only child," she said. "When I finished Oakland High School, I stayed in Maryland, going to Hood College in Frederick, then to Towson University for a year. I was interested in art, but leaned more toward history and literature. I graduated with a teaching degree, but I've never used it. I then went to Baltimore and drifted into interior decorating."

"A thumbnail sketch," Jeffrey said. "Your whole life condensed into less than two minutes."

"There was no point in dragging it out."

"Somewhere between Oakland and Tucson, something must have happened that made you afraid of relationships," Jeffrey quizzed.

Carla frowned. She looked down at her coffee cup, picked it up and sipped. Then she said, "I had the usual number of dates in high school and college. I wasn't exactly a wallflower. But,—I'd rather not talk about it."

"I had hoped you were going to give me the complete story," Jeffrey encouraged. "How am I going to know the real Carla, if you don't tell me everything? It seems like I am pushed aside every time I get near you. Am I using the wrong mouthwash?"

She smiled a little, barely turning up the corners of her mouth. "Of course not."

"Then, what happened? What made you like this?"

"My past life is none of your business, you know."

"I agree."

After sipping some coffee, Carla said, "If you really have to know, while I was living in Baltimore, I met a law student. His name was Peter Meade. We dated once in a while, then we —." She drew in her breath and let it out slowly. "Then, we started going steady. We got along so well." She looked at Jeffrey, and then looked away. "We had been dating for about two years when we decided to get married. We were engaged about a year and married just after he passed his bar exam. We honeymooned in the Bahamas and then he started working for a small law firm in town and I worked in interior decorating. Things seemed to be going so well for us for several years. Suddenly, one night, he told me it was over. He said he didn't want me any more, that he had found someone else. I—I felt like my life had ended. I didn't know what to do, what to think. I just stopped making plans for the future and tried to pick up the pieces of my life so that I could go on after our divorce."

"It must have been difficult," Jeffrey said.

"It was. We lived in a small town, where everyone knows your business."

"Did this guy stay in town?"

"No, he moved away. I've never seen him, nor heard from him again." Carla looked around. They were the only people in the dining room. A server was standing in the doorway to the kitchen, looking at them. Carla smiled at her and got up from the table. "I think the lady wants to clear our table," she said.

The server went to the cashier's desk. Jeffrey followed her and paid the check. He and Carla left the restaurant and started back to the adobe house.

"So, what did you do after this guy left?" Jeffrey asked.

Carla didn't answer at once. After a moment she said, "For a while I didn't do anything. I tried to continue my life as though nothing had happened. I acted like I was programmed. I had a job. I went to work every morning and came home to my little apartment every evening. My social life almost didn't exist anymore. I had been going around in a couple's world, but now I was single. Couples don't like to have singles around," she sighed.

Jeffrey turned his head toward her for a moment. "I know. Did you love him a lot?"

"I thought I did. Now, I'm not so sure."

"Did you keep working after he left?"

"Our divorce was uncontested and after a few months, I began to accept he was really gone. I gave up my job and left Baltimore and went back to my home town of Oakland. But I didn't fit into that world any longer either. My aunt had adjusted to my being away and wanted to enjoy her freedom. She didn't say anything, but felt that I was in the way. She had never liked Peter, so I think she was glad he wasn't in my life any longer. But she was there for me when I was growing up."

Carla and Jeffrey stopped at a corner and waited for a green light. Then they continued walking toward the adobe house.

"So you came to Tucson then?" Jeffrey asked.

"Yes. After I'd given myself a chance to adjust and figure out which direction my life was going to take. Saul Watkins was now teaching at the University of Arizona. I'd been in his English literature class at Towson, Maryland. So I decided to come out here and take some courses at the U of A. I got a job with an interior decorator shortly after I arrived. About two years ago I started my own company. Then I bought my townhouse. Without Saul, I'd never have had the courage to come here and do all that. By then, he had quit teaching and had started his antiques business in Nogales.

"Saul Watkins. Isn't he a little old for you?"

"Saul's only fifty. Oh, I see what you're thinking. Saul's just a good friend."

"I'm glad." Jeffrey's voice was low and deep.

"Losing Peter was bad enough, but what hurt most was that I felt he had just grown tired of me."

"Believe me; I would never have grown tired of you. You'd always be a special part of my life."

They had arrived at the old house. As they stood there, Carla on the steps and Jeffrey on the sidewalk, he said, "I suppose you'll spend the afternoon here."

"No," Carla said, "I'm going back to my office. I have some catching up to do. There are still two small decorating jobs that aren't finished and I'm waiting for some furniture to arrive." She turned her head toward the front wall of the old adobe house. Looking at the old door and the small windows, "I wish I could do this sort of thing, restoring old buildings all the time. It would be fun researching their history and restoring them to their original condition."

"You mean you didn't enjoy decorating my house?" Jeffrey asked.

"That was different. I had no interference. You let me do my own thing, but most jobs aren't like that. People want things that don't fit with the rest of my decorating theme. And you have to go along with their wishes. After all, it is their house and they are paying you. You can make suggestions, but the final decision is theirs," she noted, smiling.

"I like the way you decorated my house," Jeffrey said. "I especially like the detail you put into the master bathroom −, that big shower −, and the apricot colored toilet paper."

Carla laughed. "That was a neat touch, wasn't it?"

"Back to this Peter Meade. You never heard from this character again?"

"No," Carla said.

"Good. Maybe there's a place for me. You see, I'm sort of an interior decorator myself," Jeffrey smiled. "I've been thinking of redoing my life and I'd like to plan it around you. Starting with dinner tonight." The wind had begun to whip the tops of the trees that lined the street.

"All right," she said.

"Good, I'll see you at six."

"Goodbye," she called as he turned and strode across the street to his pickup. Carla watched until Jeffrey drove away, then went into the adobe house and got her briefcase. She left, locking the door behind her, and went to her car.

CHAPTER 11

On the way back to her office, Carla thought about the lunchtime conversation with Jeffrey. Her life with Peter seemed so long ago, and hadn't seemed nearly as traumatic in the telling. She realized now that the greatest hurt had come from no longer being wanted. She had given herself to Peter. He had accepted her gift, taken what he had wanted, and then left her when he was no longer interested.

I'll have to be on my guard with Jeffrey, she thought. I'll keep a safe distance between us. He had indicated that he wanted to see her and that he had future plans that included her. Talk was cheap, a way of getting through a difficult moment. Still, she hoped that he was different. She had felt a spark.

At her office, Carla spent the afternoon answering messages, bringing her bookkeeping up-to-date, writing checks, and the hundred and one things needed to operate a business. When she finally had everything in order, she looked out the big front window. The wind was blowing and traffic had increased on Ft. Lowell Road.

Time to go home, Carla thought as she stood up and stretched.

Carla went into the bedroom, her body still damp

after her shower. Her hair was twisted into a knot on the top of her head. She went to the closet in the dressing room, opened the mirrored door, and looked at the clothes hanging there. Jeffrey hadn't said where they would have dinner. What should she wear? Standing there, she surveyed her wardrobe. When in doubt, be conservative, she thought. She took down a dark brown dress and laid it over a chair. She pulled open a drawer in the chest and took out a beige lace bra and matching half slip. On her knees, she went through the rows of shoes on the closet floor until she found the nut-brown high heeled sandals. She took them from their clear plastic box and set them on the floor under the chair.

Then she sat on a wicker stool, at the vanity, and pulled on pale beige pantyhose, easing them over her legs and standing to pull them over her hips. She arranged her hair and put on makeup.

After putting on the bra, slip, and the brown knit dress, she pushed her feet into the sandals and looked at herself in the mirrored door. Nodding approval at her reflection, Carla took up her brown leather handbag and a pale beige cashmere sweater. She was leaving the dressing room when she heard the doorbell.

On her way to the front door, Carla looked at the wall clock. Jeffrey was on time, it was exactly six o'clock. Carla went to the door and opened it. Jeffrey Langley stood there. "Ready to go?" he asked.

"All ready," Carla chirped, smiling up at him.

"Then, we're on our way." Carla pulled the door closed. Jeffrey tried the latch to be sure that the door was locked. Then he and Carla walked to his Mercedes. He helped her into the car and walked around to the driver's side and got in. As he backed the car out of the driveway, Carla sank back against the velvety cushioned seat and fastened her seatbelt.

"Here we go," Jeffrey said. "I hope you like this place. It's one of my favorites."

The Mercedes moved smoothly along the streets, crossing town in an easterly direction. Then turning north, he followed a street that climbed into the foothills, the pavement gradually narrowing down to a lane. Passing through an opened gate, he entered the valet parking area and stopped the car. An attendant hurried up to the car, opened the door on the passenger's side, and helped Carla. Jeffrey emerged from the car as another attendant got in and drove the car to a parking location.

Jeffrey and Carla walked up a brick path toward a wide porch which stretched across the front of the building.

"The restaurant used to be a ranch house," he said. The ranch had been started in the eighteen-eighties. But you've probably been here before and know its history."

"No, this is the first time here for me," Carla said.

"Then, it'll be my pleasure to treat you to a wonderful evening. The food is great and the service, too."

"I hope I'm properly dressed for this place," Carla said.

"Oh, it's informal. If you're wearing shoes and are

decently covered, that's all they require." They were on the porch now. The desert scenery that had quickly darkened was bathed with spot lights that lined the walk and shone along the edge of the porch. The door opened, letting out a shaft of light. The maitre d' greeted them. "Good evening, Madam, Sir. Do you have reservations? Oh, Mr. Langley. I didn't recognize you for a moment. Your table is ready, sir." he said. "Ma'am, right this way."

"We're early," Jeffrey apologized.

"Only a few minutes, but that's quite all right. Just follow me." The maitre d' led the way to the main dining room. It was a large room with a stone fireplace at one end and a row of windows looking out onto the porch. Carla could see the string of lights, like topazes, that marked the walkway.

They were seated at a table near the fireplace and menus were placed in front of them. A waiter came to the table and took their orders for cocktails. While they waited for their drinks, Carla looked around the room. There were only a few other guests. "This room will be full in another half hour," Jeffrey said.

Carla ran her hand over the red linen cloth that covered the square table. The napkins were dark blue bandanas. The glasses and stainless silverware patterns were early Colonial. It was a pleasant room with wide planked floors and white plastered walls. Paintings of cowboys and cattle herds decorated the walls. The windows, with no curtains, looked out on the night. "The nighttime view overlooking Tucson is really striking," Jeffrey said.

"Yes, I can see that," Carla said as she hugged herself. What a wonderful place. The warmth from the fire burning in the hearth made her feel relaxed. She sighed, and then smiled at Jeffrey.

A man, wearing dark brown western cut pants and a tan western style shirt, brought their drinks. Carla lifted her glass of white zinfandel and tapped it against Jeffrey's martini.

"This calls for a toast," he said. "Here's to all things good and wonderful."

She smiled. "That could cover a large territory."

"We'll let our imaginations run wild," he said, grinning. He sipped his martini.

Carla looked at him, and then sipped her wine.

"Did your imagination run wild?" he asked, a smile starting at the corners of his mouth.

Carla blushed as she realized she would have to be careful of what she imagined when he was around. He could see directly into her mind.

Jeffrey ordered dinner for them. First came crab stuffed mushroom caps, and then a watercress soup with thin, buttery homemade cheese wafers was served. This was followed by a salmon mousse. The main dish of the evening soon appeared: a thick steak that was rare inside, but charred to perfection on the outside. The waiter served it on a platter and carved portions for each of them. The steak was accompanied by tender, crisp vegetables and delicate whole wheat rolls with a small dish of whipped butter.

Carla didn't really have room for dessert, but she made the extreme sacrifice and ate a small portion of fresh pears and apples with a wedge of a mild French cheese. Wines of several types had accompanied their leisurely meal.

Over hot black coffee and amaretto, she and Jeffrey continued their talking. Small talk, nothing of importance. It was pleasant sitting at the table near the fireplace. The quiet buzz of voices filled the room. Carla felt as though she was in a dream world.

The waiter interrupted her daydreaming as he put the dinner check on the table. Jeffrey paid, and it was time to leave. He rose from his chair and came around to where she was sitting. Pulling back her chair, she stood up. As he helped her into her cashmere sweater, Carla shivered.

They left the candle-lit room, went down the narrow hall to the wide front door, and stepped out into the cool mountain air.

"Where to?" Jeffrey asked as he helped her into the Mercedes which the attendant had delivered to the foot of the brick walk.

"Home." She sat back.

"Your home or mine?"

"Mine, of course." She sighed, "I have work to do tomorrow."

"So do I, but it's still early. We could go dancing somewhere. Or take in a late movie. Or we could go to my place?"

"Sorry," Carla said.

"Cruel woman. I'll complain to the management."

"No use. It's company policy. Besides, I have to get my beauty rest."

"No need for that," he said, as the car began to move down the drive.

When they reached the road, Carla said, "I told you the story of my life. How about your life story?" She turned her head and looked at him.

His eyes on the road, he said, "Not much to tell. Well, to start with, I'm thirty-six."

Carla smiled. "I was wondering. Go on."

"Do you mind, that I'm so much older than you?"

"Only by four years," she said.

"You seem so much younger."

"Just your imagination," she said. "Where did you grow up?"

"Well, I was born in New Mexico and lived on a ranch. But I moved to St. Louis. Near St. Louis, actually."

"You don't seem like a cowboy."

"Oh, but I was once. I went to a boarding school when I was nine, but returned home, to the ranch, during weekends, holidays, and summers. My mother had died. My father —uh, he died and I went to live with relatives in St. Louis. When it came time to go to college, I went to the University of Missouri."

"Did you study agriculture?"

"No, business administration. You see, my father wanted me to eventually take over the ranch when he couldn't run it any longer. So after finishing college, that's what I did. I took over everything, and then went on from there."

"And now you spend your time running back and forth across the country."

"Yes."

"Married?"

"No."

"Divorced?"

"No, I've never married."

"And the ranch at Dragoon?" Carla asked. "Is that part of the family empire?"

"No. That was my own idea. I bought it about seven years ago. I have a manager on it. He keeps things running. I spend as much time there as possible, but I leave the business end of it to him."

Carla watched his face in the glow of a street light when they stopped at an intersection. His profile was sharply etched. His eyes were on the road ahead. "You don't stay in any one place for very long, do you?" she asked.

"I'm flexible. If I had a reason to spend most of my time in Tucson, I could rearrange my schedule."

"I—I didn't mean that," Carla stammered. They were nearing Saguaro Square. Jeffrey pulled into the narrow lane and then into her driveway, shutting off the Mercedes' engine.

He unfastened his seat belt and inched toward her. His arm went around her shoulders. "You're sweet," he whispered in her ear. Jeffrey's arm was drawing her closer, his fingers gripping her shoulder. Warmth spread through her.

"Please," she protested. Jeffrey released her, leaning past to open the car door. After he got out of the Mercedes and held her door open, they walked to the front of the house. He took the key from her hand and unlocked the front door, and turning the handle, he pushed it open. Jeffrey put his arm around her waist as they entered the house. Inside the living room, he continued to keep his arm around her. Handing her the door key, she put it in her handbag and laid it on the hall table. Jeffrey was standing behind her now. Carla stiffened.

"I'm going home. There's plenty of time for us to get better acquainted, so don't worry. I want to see you again, but I won't rush you. I'm off to St. Louis tomorrow, and then I'll be in New York for a few days. I'll be back in Tucson, I don't know just when, but I'll call you." He pulled her into his arms and kissed her. "Wait for me, Carla." She watched as he opened the door and went out into the night, closing the door behind him. She heard his tires squeal on the pavement as he drove away.

A week had gone by when Jeffrey finally called. She was sitting at the desk in her office at Design for You. It was late afternoon and the sun had already sunk behind the buildings across the street. She had a lot to do before she could leave the office. She had to decide on wallpaper pattern for the den at the Robinson house, one of her clients. And the draperies had to match one of the colors in the paper. Why wallpaper? She preferred painted walls for the Robinson house, but Mrs. Robinson insisted on wallpaper. She opened another sample book and turned the large pages slowly, examining the samples, running her fingers over them.

The sound of the ringing phone pierced the stillness. Carla picked up the phone with her left hand while she turned a page in the sample book with her right hand.

"Design for You," she answered. "May I help you?"

"Yes.   I need another viewpoint on a serious problem. My design for life seems to be all wrong." The voice at the other end was low, reverberating.

"Jeffrey?" Carla closed the sample book.

"Hello, Carla. It's me."

"Where are you?"

"Unfortunately, I'm in New York."

Carla felt her heart go back into place. "Oh, no. So far away," she said.

"You sound as though you've missed me," Jeffrey said.

"Yes, I have," she admitted.

"Why don't you hop on a plane and fly here? If you leave now, you could be here by early morning."

"Are you completely mad?" she asked.

"I don't think so."

"I have a business to operate, Jeffrey. And it's as important to me as yours is to you."

"Hey, calm down. I didn't mean to imply that it isn't. But I miss you."

"Then, why don't you hop on your plane and come out to Tucson?   You'd be here by mid-morning tomorrow, Arizona time."

"Ah, my dearest Carla, you made your point. Commerce. It's the curse of mankind."

Carla laughed. The sound of his voice over the telephone had brightened her day.

"Do you know how long it's been since I last saw you, Carla?"

"About a week," she said.

"I think of you all the time."

"Even while you're cranking out business and turning the wheels of industry?" She heard him laugh.

"Even then. I try to not let industry interfere too much. Carla, I'm stuck here in New York until Saturday. I'll fly out of here then and I'll see you late Saturday morning." Carla didn't answer. "Carla, are you there? Will I be able to see you?"

"Yes. Shall I meet you at the airport?"

"That would be a great idea, but my ranch foreman is going to meet me. I have to go to the ranch too. Hey, why don't you go with me?"

Carla thought for a minute. "I don't know."

"Do you have anything planned for the weekend? You could go to the ranch with me and spend the rest of the weekend there."

"I don't think that would be a good idea."

"I could pick you up at your place after I arrive Saturday morning. We could spend the day at the ranch and then I'd bring you back home after dinner."

"All right. I'll be waiting," she said.

"You won't need any fancy clothes. It's a working ranch."

Their plans made, they then talked about the restoration project at the adobe house. Carla reported on the progress thus far.

"I've been telling a friend here in New York about your work," Jeffrey said. "There might be another job of the same type coming up. You'll be considered for it."

"Thanks. Wouldn't that be fun? To go around, all over the world, restoring old buildings?"

"As long as your work didn't take you away from me for very long at a time. Well, I've got to get busy. 'Bye. See you on Saturday." A click, then silence. Carla put her phone on the desk and hugged herself. It seemed like a very long time until Saturday.

CHAPTER 12

Carla awoke early Saturday morning. She usually slept late on weekends, but today she was awake at six o'clock. She got out of bed, hurried to the bathroom, and let the warm water of the shower rush over her, making her body tingle. After she had dried herself, combed her hair, and dressed in Levis and an old tee shirt, with no make up and her hair now wrapped in a braid, she went to the kitchen.

She took two eggs from the refrigerator and scrambled them. Having made whole grain toast and instant coffee, she ate her breakfast while perched on a high stool at the kitchen counter. As she was eating, Carla glanced at the wall clock. It wouldn't be long until Jeffrey arrived. She cleared away the remains of her breakfast and put the used dishes and silverware in the dishwasher.

As she walked to the living room, thoughts of Jeffrey filled her mind. She thought about the way he looked that day in the master bathroom of his house on Secret Canyon Drive. She had mistaken him for a cowboy. She laughed at her underestimation.

Carla moved her hand over the top of the end table by the sofa, remembering how Jeffrey had looked that day when he came into the adobe house downtown. Again dressed in blue jeans, but with a cotton shirt and poplin jacket. He had looked so sexy; it had taken her breath away. Yes, she would have to admit that Jeffrey Langley was a very attractive man. She perched on the arm of the wingback chair for a moment, smiling as she remembered.

But, enough of this. Get these romantic ideas out of your head, she thought. You are going to spend the day at his ranch. Nothing more. "Will there be other people there?" she wondered. She couldn't imagine Jeffrey Langley without a crowd around him. But, what if we're alone? What if there aren't any other guests? Alone with Jeffrey on a ranch in the middle of the desert. Could she handle that situation? Well, she would have to wait and see. And, she thought, if she refused to go to the ranch with him, she might never see him again.

Carla was nervous. By mid-morning, her mind was working overtime with reasons why he wouldn't come. She was pacing the hall like a caged cougar when the telephone rang. That's Jeffrey. He isn't coming, she thought, as she hurried to the phone on the end table. He's still in New York. He can't get away.

She picked up the phone on the third ring. "Hi," It was Marge's cheerful voice. "Want to do something tonight? Something exciting and devilish, like dinner and a movie?"

"Oh, Marge, I'm sorry. I'm waiting for someone."

"Ooh, sounds exciting. Do I know this someone?"

"You haven't met him yet. It's a former client that I've told you about before, the guy who owns the house on Secret Canyon Drive, Jeffrey Langley."

"Oh, that someone. How can one girl get so lucky? It must be your shampoo. Tell me, what brand do you use? I'll dash out and buy a case of it." Marge laughed.

"Where are you going? To an elegant place to dine, then dancing until dawn? Tell Aunt Marge."

"No, no, no. He's coming in from New York, and will be here any minute. Then we're going to drive out to his ranch in Texas Canyon."

"Oh, Carla, how romantic. What have I been doing wrong? Nobody ever takes me to his ranch. How long will you be gone?"

"Only for the day."

"I'll hang up, just in case he's trying to call you from the airport. Have a wonderful time, and take care. All alone with Jeffrey Langley in the middle of Texas Canyon. Wow!"

"Oh, we won't be alone. There's sure to be other people around."

"Don't count on it. If you have to holler for help, don't expect the cows to rescue you." Marge laughed. "Have fun. 'Bye."

Carla hung up her phone and smiled.

Later, she was standing by the table in the living room when the doorbell sounded. She tried to walk casually to the front door, but her steps quickened until she was almost running. She unfastened the lock and pulled the door open.

Jeffrey stood there, dressed in a dark blue suit, his broad shoulders nearly filling the doorway. His eyes devoured her as she stood perfectly still for a moment, then moved toward him. At the same time, he moved toward her and they met in a crushing embrace. His arms encircled her waist while her arms twined around his neck as she stood on tiptoe. He lowered his head.

His mouth found hers and he increased the pressure of his arms around her.

Explosions crashed through Carla and lightening seemed to flash in her brain as they kissed. Carla could feel the thumping of her heart, as she felt the pounding of his. She had thought that she had known love before, but this man passionately holding her now was love. Her knees weakening, she wanted to be in his arms forever.

After what seemed forever, Jeffrey pushed her slightly away and looked down at her. His voice was husky as he said, "We'd better get started. There's a long drive ahead of us."

Carla put her cowboy hat on her head and picked up her handbag from an end table. "Don't forget to lock the door," he said.

As they left, Carla pulled the door shut behind them. She followed Jeffrey to the blue Ford pickup parked nearby.

"Did the foreman meet you at the airport?" Carla asked.

"Yes. He drove the truck in and a ranch hand followed with my pickup, this one. Here, let me help you." He put his hand under her elbow as she stepped up into the cab with her handbag. Then he went around to the driver's side, opened the door, and climbed in.

They drove to Campbell, across town to Interstate 10, and east toward Texas Canyon. It was a cool day. Carla rolled up the window on her side. "Cold?" Jeffrey asked, rolling up the window on his side, too.

"A little. Its fine with the windows closed. I do love riding in a truck. You can see so much more."

"This is quite different from the pickups I used to drive on the farm," he said. "No automatic transmission on those. They rode like bucking mules." He laughed and the sound filled the cab. "Pickups are practical for this part of the country, though. Especially on the back roads. You'll see what I mean when we get to the ranch. Ever been to Dragoon?"

"No, but I've heard of it."

"Dragoon is about an hour east of here. It used to be an important town. There were ranches all around it. Still are, but it's almost a ghost town now. The railroad still goes through it, but there isn't much commerce any more. Texas Canyon is a pretty location, in a valley, with mountains everywhere you look."

"Is your ranch near the town?"

"Practically touches it on one side, and the north side of the ranch backs up to Interstate 10."

They drove in silence for a while. Then Carla asked, "What did you do while you were in St. Louis and New York?"

"I wasn't on a pleasure jaunt, if that's what you're thinking. I worked, everyday. It got to be a bore. I was looking forward to getting back to Arizona, — and you." He took his eyes off the road for a second and looked at her.

"I missed you while you were gone," Carla said. "Silly, isn't it? I hardly know you."

"You're going to get to know me really well. You'll learn all about me. I'm planning on it." He laughed softly, his eyes on the road.

They were now east of Tucson, climbing along the curving highway, with mountains in the distance and on both sides. The town of Benson passed by on the right, sprawled out along the highway. Then the highway began the climb toward Dragoon. As the truck moved upward toward the summit of Texas Canyon, the bright sky silhouetted the weirdly shaped rocks on either side of the road. They looked as though they had been thrown there by a mad giant long ago. Huge boulders balanced on smaller ones giving the appearance that they might topple if someone sneezed.

Boulders at Texas Canyon, AZ

Carla turned her head from side to side, trying to take in the entire splendor at once. The truck passed a yellow ranch house nestled in a ravine. For an instant Carla caught a glimpse of the water tank near it.

Almost at the summit, an exit road veered off the
Interstate on the right. Jeffrey turned the truck onto it.
He managed the hairpin curve and came to a halt at a
stop sign. A narrow road to Dragoon lay before them,
its black surface nearly covered with sand.

Highway Sign to Dragoon, AZ

Jeffrey turned to the right. The highway was above
them and the mountains of rocks were behind them.
More of the strange rock formations lay on either side of
the road, mixed with patches of grass, and groves of
mesquite trees, interspersed with cactus.

They had traveled about a mile when Jeffrey turned
left onto a road even narrower than the one they had
been traveling. He drove past mesquite and cactus
fighting for toe room between the rocks. In places, the
thorn covered branches of the prickly vegetation
reached out like wild beasts to scratch the sides of the
truck.

"We're almost there," Jeffrey said. "When we get to
that big rock—the one that looks like a whale—you'll

see the roof of the main house to the right of the gate. There, see it?"

Entrance to Texas Canyon Ranch

Carla said, "Yes, I see it." A red tiled roof peaked through the trees. The truck followed the winding lane for another mile, and then turned into a clearing.

The house in front of them was much larger than she had imagined. The mountains formed a backdrop behind it. The ground around the house had been scraped clear. A low stone wall bordered a courtyard between the parking area and the house. Jeffrey pulled into a parking place near a gateway in the wall, with a path leading to the front of the house. He helped Carla out of the truck. As he and Carla were nearing the house, the front door opened and a man, stooped and limping, came down the path to meet them.

"Hello, Charlie," Jeffrey said. "It's good to be back. Charlie, I want you to meet Carla. Carla, this is Charlie. He's the cook, butler, housekeeper —."

"And parlor maid," Charlie told her, grinning. He held out his hand to her.

"Charlie found a horse he couldn't ride. That took him out of the saddle and put him into the house," Jeffrey said.

"Yeah, and now, you're all stuck with my cookin'." Charlie haw-hawed, as he looked down at his boots.

"Although, it's actually not that bad if you're really hungry," Jeffrey said.

"Don't you believe him, ma'am. It ain't exactly gourmet, but it'll stick to your ribs. And it wasn't no horse put me in the house. It was arthritis what finished me off. Worse'n a chargin' bull." Charlie snorted as he laughed. "Come on in," he said as he limped up the path to the house. Carla followed with Jeffrey walking along behind her.

As she entered the house, she ran her fingers over the deep carving in the massive door. Inside, she looked up at the broad vigas which supported the low white plastered ceiling. The long room stretched across the front of the house. Noticing that the walls of the house were quite thick, she could see the dining room through an open door.

"Well, what do you think of it?" Jeffrey said.

"Oh, Jeffrey, it's beautiful. It looks old."

"It's been here a while. I don't know when it was built."

Carla turned around, looking at everything. "I'd love to decorate this in Territorial style, complete to the last santo and Navajo rugs."

"The Navajos never lived in this area. You'd have to hunt up an Apache rug," Jeffrey said.

"Maybe the Apaches traded with the Navajos and one of them got a good deal on a rug. They're pretty sharp, you know." Carla quipped.

Jeffrey said, "Come on; let me show you the house." He pointed to a door in the other end of the room. They went into the first bedroom opening off the hallway.

"This room shares a bath with the bedroom next to it. This is where you would sleep, if you ever stayed overnight." He looked at her and grinned. "The bathroom is in here." Jeffrey opened a door, revealing a small, modern bathroom. He turned toward her. "Not quite as fancy as the one in my Tucson house. Want to try out the tub, see if it's the right size?" he grinned.

Carla smiled and went over to the small window set deep into the thick white wall and looked out, then turned back to Jeffrey. "It's a pleasant room. The quilt on the bed looks old and is probably valuable." She could imagine that at night, the lamps on the bedside tables would cast a rosy glow over the room. "This is very nice, Jeffrey."

"My room is just across the hall here. Want to see it?" he asked as he opened the door to his bedroom. His bedroom looked much like the one he had just shown her. "By the way, Charlie's making stew for dinner tonight. Can you smell it?"

Carla nodded. "Smells good," she said. "Give me a

few minutes to wash up and then I'll join you for the rest of the tour."

"I have to change clothes. I'll be waiting in the living room." Jeffrey turned and walked down the hall.

Carla walked through the first bedroom to the bathroom. She was still wearing her hat. She hurried through a repair job of her makeup and went to the living room. Jeffrey, now dressed in old jeans and a plaid shirt, was standing in the doorway. It reminded Carla of the morning when she had first seen him.

"Come on in," he said.

"Could you show me the dining room first?" she asked. The furniture in the dining room was old; a long oak table, eight chairs, a china cabinet, and a buffet filled the space in western comfort. Decorating the walls were several paintings of cattle, horses, and cowboys.

"Mmm, something smells good," Carla said.

"Charlie really is the best cook I've ever had," Jeffrey said. "He runs the ranch, besides doing the cooking."

"He takes care of the house?" Carla asked.

"The house and the ranch, too. I can go away and know that everything is okay. Sometimes two or three months go by before I can get back here. When I do come back, it's all running fine. The books are in order and the cattle are being taken care of. I don't have to worry with Charlie on the job."

"Then, is he the manager?"

"He sure is."

At that moment, Charlie came into the dining room,

grinning.

"I overheard that. There are a few things I can still do. Learned to cook when I was a boy over a camp stove at roundups. Don't have many real old time roundups any more. And, campfire cooking is almost a thing of the past."

"I didn't know that. I thought roundups were still going on."

"Not the really big ones. And no more cattle drives. Times have changed a lot." Charlie left the room.

Jeffrey said, "Did you know that most cowboys don't permanently live on the ranches where they work? For the most part, they live in town and work on any ranch in the area that needs them. They freelance, loading their horses into trailers behind their pickup trucks, going wherever they've been hired for a job."

"That doesn't sound very practical," Carla said.

Jeffrey laughed. "Nowadays, it makes sense for the rancher as well as the hands. We only have two guys living here. Charlie and a general roustabout. Ranching has changed like everything else. It's not like a cowboy movie any more."

Jeffrey and Carla wandered into the living room. "I thought you might want to take a hike around the area, get out, and walk a little. There's a special place I'd like to show you."

"Beg pardon, Jeff," Charlie said, standing in the kitchen doorway. "I kinda thought you'd maybe want to show Miss Carla around, so I fixed y'all a picnic lunch. I'll go get it and you can take off adventurin'."

"Good idea," Jeffrey said. He turned to Carla.

"Want to do that? Go adventuring?"

"Oh, yes. Thank you, Charlie," Carla said.

A few minutes later, Jeffrey was carrying the picnic lunch as he and Carla left the house and walked down the path to a narrow dirt road that went winding up the hill. Waist high creosote bushes grew on either side of the trail. Occasionally, tall trees, still wearing their green leaves, pierced the blue sky. The quiet stillness was mesmerizing. At the top of the hill, they stood, looking out in all directions. "I can't believe this," Carla whispered. "It's so peaceful."

"Yes, you can get a lot of thinking done around here," Jeffrey said.

"Where are the cattle? I thought I'd see a lot of cows and bulls and cowboys."

"Cows prefer to stay away from people. The farther away they are from human beings, the happier they're going to be as long as they have something to eat."

"This is a beautiful spot. Looking out over all of God's creation. Think what a developer would do to this," Carla said.

"I hope a developer never sees it," Jeffrey said. "I shudder at the thought."

"With no developers, there wouldn't be much work for interior decorators. What are you doing, trying to put me out of a job?" Carla grinned. Jeffrey laughed.

"This might be a nice spot for our picnic," Carla said. "I'm hungry."

"Sure, why not. How about over here? There's even a convenient flat rock that you can use for a seat." Jeffrey walked over and set down the bag filled with their picnic lunch.

As he and Carla ate the food Charlie had prepared for them, they looked out at the peaceful scene before them. "There are some cows," she pointed with her sandwich. "Over there, in that clearing."

"Those aren't cows," Jeffrey corrected. "Those are deer. There are lots of them around here. They eat the grass meant for the cows. Boy, I've got my job laid out for me. Gotta teach you the difference between a cow and a deer," he laughed.

"Well, I'm a city girl, you know."

After Carla and Jeffrey had finished eating, he said, "There's another place I'd like to show you. We'll go back to the house and have Charlie saddle up two horses for us."

"Is Charlie able to do that sort of thing?" Carla asked. "He limps so badly."

"Oh, sure. He just can't ride any longer."

Carla and Jeffrey picked up the area around the rock, leaving no sign of their picnic lunch. Then they walked back to the ranch house. Charlie saddled two horses for them and they started riding down the hill toward the lane. Jeffrey led the way toward a grove of trees at the foot of another hill. As they rode, Carla looked at the plants and occasional cacti lining the path.

"This is more rugged looking than the area where we were earlier, she said.

"Yes, it is," Jeffrey said. "The cows like to hide out here when the guys are looking for them. They hate having to ride in, under the trees, to flush them out."

"It's beautiful, though. I like it as much as the place

where we ate our lunch," Carla said.

"We're almost at the place I wanted to show you," Jeffrey said. "Right about here. Okay, let's dismount and tie the horses to that tree." He pointed to a small tree as he got off his mount and helped Carla to get down.

"Now, let's walk up toward the top of this hill." They started walking up the steep incline, climbing for about five minutes. Panting, Jeffrey said, "Stop right here. What do you see?"

Carla looked around. "Not much," she said. "Just a grove of trees, and vines growing up the side of that wall of rocks."

"See the opening in the wall?"

"No. Oh, yes, at the bottom," Carla said.

They squeezed through the brush to the low, narrow opening. Inside, the space was about five feet high and about the width of an old fashioned telephone booth. The brown stone walls were covered with brightly painted lines, circles, and figures that might represent deer.

"Here, sit on this little bench," Jeffrey said. Carla sat on a narrow ledge of stone that formed a natural bench. "Now, look up." Handprints, in reds and yellows, covered the low ceiling.

"Oh, my goodness. It's awesome," Carla said in a hushed voice. "Who did this? Who painted this? Are they really handprints?"

"Nobody knows who did this. They sure look like handprints. It's really old. A friend of mine who's studied all this kind of thing says it goes back a long,

long time. Maybe centuries ago. Not very many people know its here, which is a good thing."

"Did you find any artifacts in here, broken pots, and such?"

"Not here, but scattered around the ranch. We found some pots and stones for grinding grain and arrowheads. The stuff went back a long, long way into times past. What Charlie and I found, we gave to the museum down the road. They kept most of it, but gave some to other museums."

"What do you suppose this space was used for?" Carla mused.

"Oh, a place to get in out of the cold, a place to sleep." He smiled, "A place to make a phone call."

"Yeah, right," Carla mocked. "Don't joke; this is such a wonderful place. Although it does look like an old fashioned phone booth."

Jeffrey reached over and patted her on the shoulder. "You really take this kind of stuff seriously, don't you?" Carla nodded.

"Well, we'd better get back to the ranch house. Just about time to eat dinner and get you back to Tucson. I can't believe how fast this day is going." Jeffrey helped Carla up from the narrow bench and brushed her off.

They squeezed through the opening and walked out into the sunlight. Carla said, "That is the most amazing place I have ever seen." She turned and looked back toward the opening, now hidden by the bushes and cactus. They walked carefully back to their horses, descending the hill they had climbed earlier. The light had changed. The cows had moved. A few lizards scurried out of the way as they mounted their horses and rode back toward the ranch house now visible at the foot of the hill they were descending.

"This has been a wonderful day," Carla said. "I had never been in this part of the state. Thank you."

"You've probably driven through it, and you've certainly flown over it. You just didn't know what was here," Jeffrey said.

They dismounted near the ranch house and Carla waited while Jeffrey took the horses back to the corral. When he came back, they walked to the porch and went inside. The smell of something wonderful filled the place. "Mmm, smells good," Carla said.

"Charlie's stew," Jeffrey said. He looked at his watch. "An early dinner and then we'll hit the road for Tucson."

"I hate to leave," Carla said.

"You don't have to. You could stay over, if you want to."

"No, I have things to do at home. Besides, I have to spend some time with my next door neighbor, Marge Jenkins. I turned down an invitation from her for today and I have to make it up to her."

"Known her a long time?" Jeffrey asked.

Carla nodded. "She was living in the townhouse next door when I moved into mine about three years ago."

Charlie came into the dining room, saw Jeffrey and Carla in the doorway, and said, "Oh, you're back. Time for supper. Stew and fixings and lots of biscuits. I hope you're hungry."

Carla said, "I'm starved. This guy walked my legs off today."

Jeffrey laughed.

Charlie said, "He's a great one for taking off across the pastures. Did he show you his telephone booth?"

"Yes," Carla said. "Fantastic!"

Charlie disappeared into the kitchen and returned with a big bowl of stew which he set on the table between the two place settings at one corner of the big table. After washing up, Carla and Jeffrey sat down and began to fill their plates. Charlie went to the kitchen and returned with biscuits, butter, and jam. He went back to the kitchen and returned immediately with a pot of coffee and a pitcher of cream. "Well, dive in. There's more where that came from. Just yell." He limped away.

"It would be nice if you could stay over sometime," Jeffrey said, between mouthfuls of stew.

"I don't know. I'd have to think about it," Carla said.

"I wouldn't bother you. Not unless you wanted me to," he teased.

Carla blushed. "I'll just eat my stew and think about what a wonderful day we've had."

Jeffrey smiled warmly at her. "Keep my offer in mind."

The sun had long gone down when they got into Jeffrey's truck and started the drive back to Tucson. By the time they reached the highway and turned left, stars perforated the black sky.

"Night seems to come quickly out here," Carla said.

"Yes, one minute it's dusk and then, wham, it's night. Oh, I was intending to ask you, how's the restoration job going on the old house in downtown Tucson?"

"It's moving right along," Carla said. "We should be finished in another month. The opening is scheduled for sometime in November. They were planning a typical Mexican Christmas, the way it would have been before Arizona was a territory of the U.S. However, they decided to move it up a month and make it just a regular reception with a walkthrough."

"Sounds great, although a Christmas party would have been better," Jeffrey said, keeping his eyes on the road. The west-bound traffic was a bit heavier now.

"Yes," Carla said. "It'll be wonderful. But, I agree with you. A Christmas season opening would have been a real hit. There'll be all sorts of VIP's there. I'm sure you'll be one of them."

"Why me?"

"Don't be modest, Mr. Moneybags," Carla said.

"I just did what I could to help."

"And it was appreciated, believe me. Without your check, they wouldn't have been able to keep going without disruptions while everyone scouted around for funds."

"Like a treasure hunt?" Jeffrey said.

"Exactly. You made the way smoother for them."

They were nearing Tucson city limits now and the traffic was becoming more congested. Jeffrey said, "I'm expecting a friend from St. Louis next week, Sydney Allen, who'll be staying at my house in Tucson. We have business to work out on a deal we're in now. I'll be going back to St. Louis for a few days with Syd, then finally back to Tucson."

"Oh," Carla said. "I guess I won't be seeing you for a while."

"I'll keep in touch. And I'll be seeing you at the adobe house downtown once in a while. If it's okay, I would like to call you now and then." They were nearing the turnoff to Houghton Road.

"Hey, I just had an idea," Jeffrey said. "Why don't we go to my house and have a drink? It's still early."

"I don't know," Carla said. "I have things to do when I get home. And I wanted to spend an hour or so with Marge, my neighbor."

"Oh, come on. Alma and Frank will probably be eating their supper. You won't be alone in the house with me, if that's what's bothering you."

"No, it's not that. Oh, alright. But just for one drink. Then you have to take me home."

"I promise."

Jeffrey exited Interstate 10, driving north on Houghton road, then west on Tanque Verde to Grant and north again on Swan. At Skyline Drive, he turned left for a short distance, and finally right toward his home on Secret Canyon Drive.

When they reached Jeffrey's house, he turned his truck into the lane and parked in the area next to the house. Carla glanced around. The new, raw edges were wearing off the house. It was beginning to look like it was part of the landscape. Alma met them at the front door.

"Good evening, Mr. Langley. Well, hello, Carla. What a surprise."

"Sorry to barge in on you unannounced, Alma," Jeffrey said. "I'll be staying over tonight. I thought it would be nice to bring Carla home with me. We're going to have a drink and then I'll drive her back to her place."

"I could fix you some crackers and cheese," Alma said. "Sandwiches and coffee? Some leftover chocolate cake?"

"I'm still stuffed from dinner at your ranch, Jeffrey. I spent the day at his ranch near Dragoon, Alma. It's such a beautiful area."

"That's nice," Alma said. "Always good to get out into the country. I'll be back in a minute with the crackers and cheese."

Carla and Jeffrey went into the den. Jeffrey poured the drinks and waited for Alma to bring the food. "What this house needs," Carla said, "is a breakfast room."

"There's the sunroom," Jeffrey said. "Why not use one corner of that?"

"Good idea. Only, it's too far from the kitchen. Oh, here comes Alma."

Alma put a tray in front of them. "Three kinds of crackers and three kinds of cheese. I hope it's enough. I can fix something more if you want?" she asked.

"No. This will be fine, Alma. Thank you," said Jeffrey.

Alma set the tray down on a little table and went back to the kitchen.

"I wish you and I could have more days like this," Jeffrey said. "I had a really good time today. Being with you is special."

Carla smiled as she bit into a piece of cheese.

"Let's do this more often," he said.

"I'd like that," said Carla.

The front doorbell sounded. "Now, who could that be?" Jeffrey wondered. Carla saw Alma pass the studio door on her way to the front entrance.

A woman's voice, low and sexy, asked, "Is Mr. Langley at home?"

"Yes, madam," Alma said.

"Tell him Sydney Allen has arrived. Well, don't just stand there, hurry up! Thank you, driver, set the bags down here."

CHAPTER 13

Carla sat, frozen at the table. Jeffrey stood up, his mouth open with surprise. "That sounds like —, but it can't be." He hurried away, leaving Carla sitting there alone.

"Sydney," Carla heard him say. "I wasn't expecting you so soon. You told me you'd arrive next Friday."

"Surprise, Jeffrey. I couldn't wait. I hope you don't mind."

"No, of course not. Oh, I'm sorry. I've messed up your hair."

"I don't mind, darling. You've messed it up before." Her laugh, low and musical, floated down the hall to Carla.

"Pay the cab driver like a good boy. Thank you, driver. Goodbye."

"Come on back to the sunroom," Jeffrey was saying. "I was just having some coffee with a friend. I just got back from the ranch, you almost missed me."

That's a woman Jeffrey's talking to, Carla said to herself. I thought Sydney was a man. She looked around the sunroom for escape. She didn't want to be here when Jeffrey came through the door with this woman. Obviously, she wouldn't expect to find Carla here. But there was no way she could escape without going through the foyer. Oh, she thought, maybe I can get to the kitchen and Alma and Frank would call a cab for her.

Carla got up and was ready to go into the kitchen

when Jeffrey came through the other door with the woman. She was almost as tall as Jeffrey. Her shoulder length blond hair brushed her cheek on one side and was swept back behind her ear on the other. Jeffrey was holding her right hand. Her long, narrow face was dominated by a full mouth now curved in a smile as she looked at Jeffrey. Then she turned her head and saw Carla.

Carla was pinned down by the look in the woman's large green eyes. They matched the jade chevron striped silk dress the woman was wearing.

"Oh—oh, have I interrupted something? You didn't say you'd have a girl hanging around," the woman said. "Well, just go on as though I'm not here. I'll go to my room." Just then Alma appeared in the kitchen doorway. The woman turned to Alma and said, "Oh, you must be the servant. Which room is mine, dear?"

Alma looked from the woman to Jeffrey. "Shall I take her bags, Mr. Langley?" she asked.

"Yes, Alma, take them upstairs. Pick out any bedroom you want, Syd. There are plenty of them to choose from."

As Sydney left the room following Alma to the stairs, she turned back and looked at Carla. Carla stared back at her. The swish of silk and the waft of expensive perfume still lingered in the room as Sydney left.

Carla thought, my world is collapsing and I can't stop it. She isn't pretty, but she has a kind of beauty. She's tall, slender, and sure of herself. Carla looked down at her own rumpled jeans and scuffed boots. She would have given anything to be freshly bathed, dressed in something feminine and stylish, and terribly expensive. What she needed was at least a fighting chance against this person in designer clothes who had invaded what Carla had come to think of as her own territory.

When he and Carla were alone, Jeffrey turned to Carla. "Now, don't get any ideas. I honestly didn't know she would be arriving this evening. She was supposed to arrive next week."

"And she really is a business colleague?"

"Yes and a friend."

"I could see that. She seems terribly friendly," Carla said icily.

"You'll like her when you get to know her."

"I doubt that I'll ever get the chance. She didn't seem too anxious to be friends. Now I know why you needed to get back to town early. Too bad you brought me here. That was a miscalculation on your part."

"Carla, you're being unreasonable. I told you, I didn't know she was coming here tonight," Jeffrey pleaded.

"I don't think I'm being unreasonable. I'd like to go home. Will you please call a cab?"

"No, I won't call a cab. I don't want you to go, and especially not like this. Why don't you stay overnight and I'll take you home in the morning."

"I can't stay here. How could I possibly stay when you have your—your —."

"Sydney is only a friend. I told you that."

"Yes. I know. You told me that. And a very dear

friend," Carla said.

"She and I have business arrangements together. Just like I do with lots of people."

"But what kind of business? That's what bothers me. I'm sorry; your arrangements with—with Sydney are ..."

I'm going to cry, Carla thought. I will not give him the benefit of knowing that he has hurt my feelings, embarrassed me, and insulted me. Carla wiped her eyes with the back of her hand. "Please call a cab; I want to go home now!" She turned toward the kitchen. "Never mind, I'll ask Alma to call a cab."

Jeffrey grabbed her arm. "I'll take you home."

"You shouldn't leave. It would be rude as you have a guest."

"Carla, cut it out or I'll spank you!"

"You wouldn't dare!" Carla shouted.

"Don't tempt me. Now, come on, let's go to the car." He released her and went out of the room, toward the front door. Carla walked along behind him, barely able to keep up.

He's angry with me, she thought. I'm not the one who barged into his home, uninvited, making rude remarks. He's got a job ahead of him if he thinks he is going to be angrier than I am right now!

Outside, Carla followed Jeffrey to the pickup. They got in and Jeffrey drove down the lane and out into Secret Canyon Drive. All the way to Skyline Drive, he was silent, watching the road. Carla stared out the windshield. They rode across town without speaking. When they were nearing Saguaro Square, Jeffrey finally broke the silence.

"You're making a mistake about Sydney and me. As I told you, she's only a friend."

Carla continued to look ahead. "But you seem to mean a lot to her."

"Only as a friend."

"You must be blind, Jeffrey. She feels a lot more for you than mere friendship. She probably has grounds for feeling that way."

"I don't give a damn how she feels or what you think!" His voice rose to a shout, filling the pickup. "She's never been anything to me but a friend. And she never will." He turned the pickup into the lane leading to Carla's townhouse. "You're the one I care about. You're the one I want to be with. Any fool should be able to see that."

"I thought that my life could be different now," Carla said as the car moved over the speed bumps in the road. "I thought the past was over, forgotten, and that I could start something new with you. But it seems I was wrong."

"You haven't heard a word I've been saying." He stopped the pickup at the entrance to the carport. "You've made a big mistake, Carla."

"That's what I said. I made a mistake. I had thought —."

"No, you're throwing away something wonderful, precious, to both of us."

As she got out of the truck, she said, "I'll never make this mistake again, Jeffrey. Believe me, twice is enough." She slammed the door and didn't look back as she walked to the front of her townhouse, took her keys from her pocket, and unlocked the door. She started to go inside.

"Wait," Jeffrey called. "You forgot your handbag." She stood there, the door halfway open. He came up to her and gave her the handbag. "Carla, please, let's not part like this."

She looked at him. In her mind she imagined Peter walking through another door, in another time, and she heard her own voice saying the words Jeffrey had just said. Sydney Allen had walked into Jeffrey's house tonight and stood between them. Things were different now. They could never be the same again. Let Jeffrey suffer now as she had suffered when Peter had walked out of her life.

She turned toward the door. "I'm going in now." She heard Jeffrey exhale in exasperation. She didn't turn back.

Carla waited inside, by the front door, now closed and locked. She heard the pickup backing away. Jeffrey was leaving and would never return. She had made the decision for both of them.

CHAPTER 14

The dawning day was a spectacular Sunday morning. Another beautiful October day, Carla yawned as she looked out the window of her bedroom. She got out of bed, stretched and went to the bathroom to take a shower. The warm water poured over her. She had not slept well. She remembered her anger with Jeffrey last night and that woman coming into the house, acting like she owned it. She remembered the way Sydney had looked down at her with contempt.

Carla combed her hair and put on lipstick. After dressing in old jeans and a well worn tee shirt, she went through the townhouse to the kitchen. What will I have for breakfast today, she wondered, maybe an omelet? I haven't had one in a long time. I don't really care what I have. And, I won't think about last night. Hey, I have an idea. I'll call Marge and ask her if she wants to go to El Hombre for eggs and sausages. That way I won't be alone thinking about that horrible woman.

She went to the living room, opened the blinds, and looked out. No cars were passing in front of the house. It was still early. Soon neighbors would be driving past on their way to church.

Carla picked up her phone and called Marge. A sleepy voice answered the third ring. "Hello."

"Hi, Marge, it's me, Carla."

"Oh, Carla. I kinda thought you'd be staying over at that guy's ranch."

"No. It was just for the day."

"Did you have a good time? Is it a real ranch? Cows and all?"

"Yep, a real ranch. There were a lot of cows, and horses, too. We walked all over the place and had a picnic lunch. That guy, Jeffrey, remember? He drove me back to his house on Secret Canyon Drive. Alma made coffee for us."

"Oh? And how are Alma and Frank?"

"I didn't see Frank. He was in the kitchen, but Alma looked just fine."

"All alone all day with a multimillionaire. How lucky can some girls get?" Marge sighed.

"Well, a millionaire, yes. I don't know about the 'multi-' part," Carla said. "But, the reason I called was to ask you if you want to go to El Hombre for breakfast."

"Oh, what a great idea. Then I won't have to fix breakfast. How should I dress? I'm still in my nightgown."

"Well, I'm afraid that's just a wee bit too informal. I'm wearing old jeans and tee shirt. It's just about the right thing to wear to El Hombre."

"Okay, jeans it is. How long 'til you're ready to leave?"

"I'm ready now."

"Give me fifteen minutes. I'll come over to your place."

"Okay, I'll be waiting," Carla said.

While she waited for Marge, Carla took out her Day Planner and checked her appointments for the coming week. The plans for her new customer were coming along nicely. The furniture had been chosen. There was still some problem with the draperies for the living room and study. The color wasn't exactly what the customer wanted. Carla sighed. The woman had changed the color three times.

The work on the old adobe house in downtown Tucson was going nicely. She would hear from Professor Cantrell this coming week. Saul Watkins had been in touch with her. The furniture for the large bedroom in the adobe house would arrive in another two weeks. The other bedrooms would be left bare and would not be available to visitors.

A knock on the door took Carla's attention away from her notes. She closed her Planner and went to the door. When she opened it, Marge was standing there dressed in immaculate black jeans and a turquoise tee shirt. She was wearing black canvas sandals.

"You look great," Carla told her. She looked down at her own battered clothes. "You make me look like a walking rag bag."

"You look fine. I'm a little bit overdressed, but it is Sunday."

"I know what you mean," Carla said. "Hard to outgrow our early traditions, isn't it? Always dress up on Sunday." She picked up her tote bag and closed the door behind her. "I remember, on Sunday we had to go to Sunday School and be properly dressed and sometimes wear a hat. I didn't dare depart from those rules until I was eighteen years old and in college." She and Marge laughed.

The drive to El Hombre was along quiet city streets.

"I love Sundays," Marge said, "mainly because there isn't as much traffic. And I love eating at El Hombre. It's a crazy place. It's hard to imagine that eating outdoors with a bunch of metal tables and chairs under a long, corrugated roof could be so popular. No frills, no décor, just space and wonderful food."

They had reached El Hombre. Carla drove up to the curb and parked. The lot was full of cars and there was a line of customers in front of the kitchen trailer. Marge and Carla joined them. Everyone was talking, turning to speak to the people behind them, or calling to the people ahead of them. The dress code was everything from Sunday best to old work clothes. Senior citizens, young people, children all stood in line, waiting to give their orders to Tony Jimenez.

When Carla and Marge reached the front of the line, Tony welcomed them. "And what will you have this morning, Ms. Jenkins?" he asked.

"I'll have two eggs over easy, with ham and tortillas," Marge said.

"Tortillas don't go with American ham and eggs, silly," Carla said.

"I don't care. That's what I want. Can I do that, Tony?"

"You can have anything you want, just so long as I can fix it." He smiled at the two women. Carla thought Tony's smile could make anyone's day better.

"And you, Ms. Meade?" he asked.

"Give me a ham omelet and twelve grain toast."

"You got it," Tony said. He yelled the two orders to the cook and smiled at the women as they moved away toward the tables under the long roof in the middle of the lot.

They found a table with two empty places side by side. "What a miracle," Marge said. "Two places together."

"You don't find that very often on a Sunday morning. Tony does a good business," Carla said.

"Yes, he does," Marge said.

They spoke to the people on either side of them and across the table from them. A boy brought coffee, cream, and sugar. Carla sighed and picked up her coffee container. She sipped the strong brew and sighed again. "Delicious coffee on a beautiful Sunday in a wonderful town," she said. "Who could ask for more? What are your plans for the day?" she said to Marge.

"I'll do some work when I get home. Get caught up on my orders." Marge was self-employed and worked from home. She designed and sold handbags and totes. "I have two new orders. One goes to Alabama and the other to California. And you, what are you going to do when you get home?"

"I have to plan next week's schedule. I may go to the office to work."

"You sound kind of down. Has something happened? I thought things were going along great with that guy, Jeffrey."

Just then their breakfast was served. When the young waiter had left, Carla said, "Jeffrey and I are finished. It's over, almost before it began. We went to his house on Secret Canyon Drive when we got back from the ranch. Just as we were starting to relax with a drink and some appetizers, his girlfriend arrived."

"Oh, no," Marge said.

CHAPTER 15

Sydney Allen has been settled into the house on Secret Canyon Drive for two days now, Carla thought, while working in her office. There were some last minute changes in the arrangement of furniture in the restoration project in downtown Tucson. The grand opening would take place at the end of the month. Carla was looking at the floor plans of the old adobe house when the phone rang. It was Alma Ebers.

"Hello, Alma. How are things going?"

"Oh, Carla. It's terrible. Everything's terrible. That woman —. Oh, dear, I hope she can't hear me."

"Is she still there?"

"Oh, yes. Very much so. She's unpacked three bags and settled herself in for the long haul, I'm afraid. Carla, she's called another interior decorator. She—you won't believe this—she says the house is impossible. Nothing's the right color. She doesn't like the furniture. Says she's going to throw it out and get all modern stuff."

"Oh, dear. What does Mr. Langley say about all that?"

"He's not here. He's in St. Louis."

"Why don't you call him?"

"Oh, Frank and I can't do that. We're just employees here. It isn't our house. Our hands are tied."

"Call him, Alma! If he knows about this woman's actions and approves, then there is nothing anyone else can do. But maybe he doesn't know."

"She's just taken over and is running things like it's her own house. Oh, dear. What if she fires Frank and me? If she does what she wants to do to the house, then she could fire us."

"If you don't call Jeffrey Langley, then I will!" Carla said. "But it's not my place to do that. You're the one who has to do it, you or Frank."

"Alright, I'll call him," Alma said.

"Let me know as soon as you've talked to him," Carla said.

"Alright."

Carla continued working, but her mind was not on the job in front of her. She kept thinking about the house on Secret Canyon Drive and that woman, Sydney Allen.

It was Wednesday night and Carla was waiting for her friends: Marge, Anna, and Pearl. They were going to pick her up and go to a melodrama at the Playhouse on East Broadway. Pearl was to drive.

She saw Pearl's car drive up and park in the driveway when the phone rang. She picked it up. "Hello. Oh, Alma." The doorbell rang. "Just a minute, Alma. I have to get the door. It's one of my girlfriends."

She hurried to the door and opened it. "Hi, Pearl. Just a minute. I have someone on the phone." Pearl nodded and went back to her car. Carla could see Anna sitting in the front seat with her. Back on the phone, Carla said, "What's up, Alma?"

"Sydney Allen is gone. She left this morning in a huff."

"Tell me about it."

"Well, I called Mr. Langley, like you told me to. He got that woman on the phone and I guess, from the look on her face, he really gave it to her. She took his call in the front hall and I was standing in the living room. I could hear her talking—or rather, listening."

"And then what happened?"

"She put down the phone and went upstairs. In a little, she called downstairs and talked to Frank. He went up to her room and came down with her luggage."

"No kidding? I wonder what Mr. Langley said."

"She told Frank to drive her to the airport."

"He should have told her to get a taxi," Carla said.

"He did. That's what he told her. Frank said he couldn't leave the house because he had a job underway and couldn't leave it. Not true, but that's what he told her."

"Good for him. Did she call a cab?"

"Yes. She was angry, but she called a cab. She was gone from the house in less than half an hour."

"Is everything all right there?" Carla said.

"Just fine now."

"She didn't mess the house up too much?"

"She moved a few pieces around, but we've put them back the way they were. Mr. Langley stopped her before she sold a bunch of stuff and bought something different," Alma said.

"I'm glad it's all over and that things have calmed down. Well, thank you for calling, Alma. I'm going to a play with my girlfriends. They're waiting for me."

"Have fun."

"Bye, Alma. Say hello to Frank for me," Carla said.

Carla went outside, locked the door behind her, and walked over to Pearl's car.

"Sorry I kept you waiting. I had a call from Alma Ebers."

"Oh? Is everything all right at the big house?" Marge asked.

"It is now. Remember I told you that a so-called friend of Mr. Langley arrived and was making herself at home?"

"Oh, yes. I remember," Marge said.

"Well," Carla said, "she's been acting like it was her house, rearranging things and all. Then, she started making plans to have the place completely redone. Alma called me, all upset. I told her to call Jeffrey Langley. She did and now the woman is gone."

"She just up and disappeared, just like that?"

"No, Jeffrey—uh, Mr. Langley told her to get out, and she did."

"Uh huh," Marge said. "No more obstacles in your path, eh?" Pearl started the engine of her car and they began to move down the street and out of Saguaro Square.

The traffic was unusually heavy for a weekday evening. When they arrived at the little theater on

Broadway, Carla was ready for something to eat. Pearl parked the car in the big lot and the four women walked over to the Playhouse. A big sign on the marquee announced "Alien Takeover." They joined the line of theater goers and before too long they were seated near the stage.

In a few minutes a young woman in a tight fitting coverall with a helmet on her head took their order for tacos and milk shakes. Another young woman, dressed in the same manner, brought a large bag of popcorn.

The show began with a loud piano rendition of classical music that gave the impression of open skies, rolling planets, and distant stars. Then the curtains parted and a man in a bright orange space suit came to the front of the stage and, sneering and grinning, began to hurl insults at the crowd. Amid much booing, he shook a threatening fist at the audience, sneered again, and left the stage. Two hours of hilarity followed.

After the show, Pearl, Marge, Anna, and Carla left and began the drive back to Saguaro Square. "That was some show," Carla said.

"It was hilarious. I'm not quite sure what it was all about, but I enjoyed it," Pearl smiled as she recalled some of the comedy.

"An evening well spent," Carla said. "But, I think I've had my fill of popcorn for a while."

"Carla, will everything be all right between you and Mr. Langley now?" Marge asked with concern as Pearl turned into Saguaro Square.

"I don't know what you mean," Carla said looking away.

"Don't try to fool me, Carla. I know you and he are crazy about each other."

"He is only a client, a past client at that."

"You were working with him on that adobe house thing. You went to his ranch. You went to his house on Secret Canyon Drive. Only a client ...yeah, I don't think so."

"I don't want to talk about it," Carla said.

"Okay, okay. Sorry," Marge said.

They had arrived at Marge's townhouse. Pearl pulled into the drive and Marge and Carla got out. "Goodnight," they all called to one another.

"I really had a fun time tonight, Marge. I'm sorry I was so grouchy on the way home."

"Don't worry about it. And don't let things get you down. You know what I mean."

"Yes, I know. Thanks, Marge. Goodnight."

Carla walked over to her townhouse, unlocked the door, and went inside.

CHAPTER 16

October came to an end, another page torn from her calendar. Carla wondered where the days had gone. November had come in, cool and dry. The usual migration of winter visitors was returning to Arizona, escaping the Midwest where temperatures had already dipped to freezing. Two of Carla's past clients were "snowbirds."

Carla tried to keep her mind off Jeffrey. He had called several times the week after that unforgettable Sunday when Sydney Allen had forced her way into his house. Carla refused to talk to him, hanging up after only a few words. He had written twice, once from St. Louis and once from New York. She had ripped open the envelopes, hurriedly read the messages, and torn the letters into shreds.

If Jeffrey thought she was going to forgive and forget, he was mistaken. She might even regret spending the rest of her life alone, as he had pointed out in one letter. That was a possibility, but Carla didn't care. Before he had come into her life, she had been resolved to loneliness. She could do it again. She recalled how life had been before she had met him. She had kept busy with her work, but the nights were a different story. She didn't look forward to that again, even though that was how things had to be. She would survive.

She shook her head to clear her brain of these thoughts. Sitting at the desk in her office, she pulled a large envelope toward her. It contained the plans of the adobe house in the downtown historical district. The restoration was going nicely. A meeting had been scheduled with Saul Watkins for today. Saul was going to supply several pieces of furniture from the time period when the house had been built. He had just recently located the furniture in Mexico City.

Carla returned from a hasty lunch at the corner eatery. As she reached her office, she saw Saul leaning against the door. When he saw her, he smiled.

"Hi," he said. "Nice lunch?"

"Great. I went to the little Mexican eating place at the corner, El Hombre."

"Oh, yes, the open air place."

"Come on in," Carla said as she unlocked the door and pushed it open. She sat down at her desk and motioned for Saul to sit across from her. He looked like a friendly bear, his bulk filling the chair, stretching his tweed jacket to the limit.

"Saul, it's good to see you."

"You've been neglecting me, darling. You haven't been down to Nogales to see me for ages. All those pretties sitting there. Those are gems of Mexico, just waiting for you to bring to Tucson. I can see you don't love me any more. If you did, you wouldn't be able to stay away so long." His voice was a low deep base, somewhere inside that huge chest.

"You're just saying that because you have some stuff you can't sell and I look like the right person to take it off your hands."

Saul laughed, "How did you ever guess?"   He

opened his briefcase and removed some photographs and pushed them across the desk to Carla. "I found these recently in a townhouse of a former viceroy who lived in Mexico City, c. 1650. They are authentic, I've checked them out. Look at those lines. This was the viceroy's personal desk. Isn't it a beauty? It's a steal at the price. I'm giving it to you, Carla. A gift."

"You mean it's free?"

"Well, practically free. The price is on the back."

Carla turned the photo over and looked at the figure. She nodded. "That's a good price, Saul. But isn't it rather ornate for the restoration project?"

"Perhaps, but I had to show it to you. Maybe you can use it somewhere else. Keep it in mind. Now, this." He pushed another photograph toward her.

"This is more like it," Carla said, studying the small, plain writing table in the photograph. She turned the picture over and noted the price. "I think the price is right on this one too. It would look great in the adobe house."

"I've already taken the liberty of having it delivered. It should be there the next time we go to the old house. Oh, and look at this." Saul pushed another photo across the desk. Carla picked it up and studied it. It was an old bed, small and plain with no ornamentation. "Isn't it beautiful? You must take it, you must."

There was something familiar about that bed. What was it? A memory came into her mind. Had she seen a bed similar to that somewhere? No, it was just her imagination.

She finished looking at the photographs that Saul

had pushed across her desk. He was a great salesman. She had to stay firm. When he had finished his sales pitch, she asked, "Where are you staying in town?"

"I'm not staying. I'm going back to Nogales tonight after dinner. I've been invited to Jeffrey Langley's house. He's having some people in for dinner. Why don't you go with me? He told me to bring a date, if I liked."

Carla had been smiling. At the mention of Jeffrey's name, a frown replaced the smile.

"What's the matter? Did I say something wrong?"

"No. No, it's nothing. I—I can't go to Mr. Langley's house with you, sorry."

"Another date?"

Carla nodded. Think of something quick, she told herself. "I—I'm having dinner with a neighbor, Marge Jenkins. And some of my other girlfriends. It's the monthly meeting of the Shufflettes."

Now I'll have to call Marge and invite her over for dinner, she thought. Otherwise I'll get caught up in this lie.

Saul's hearty laughter shook his body. "The *what* did you say?"

"The Shufflettes … and you can stop laughing. It's my bridge group. We meet once a month and it's my turn to have them at my house. Tonight."

"I thought you said you were going to have dinner with this Marge person."

"Well —."

"I think you invented the whole thing. Not the Shufflettes. Only a group of women would come up with a moniker like that. But I don't think you're going to play bridge tonight, and I don't think you're having dinner with Marge what's-her-name." Saul shook his head. "I think it's all an excuse to get out of having to see Jeffrey. For some reason, you don't want to go to his house, do you?"

"You're right about the dinner with Marge and the bridge game," Carla confessed. "I invented that. And you're right about Jeffrey Langley, too. I don't ever want to see him."

"That bad, eh?" Carla nodded, looking down at her hands. "You know what I think? I think you should face whatever is bothering you and go to Langley's get-together with me," Saul said. "Be my date. Now, doesn't that sound exciting?" He stood and pulled her to her feet, held her at arm's length and asked, "Hmm?"

"I know that you're an ex-professor and that you're a slick dealer in Mexican antiques, but I didn't know that you're also a psychiatrist, Saul," Carla laughed. The picture of her and Saul as a dating couple was so ridiculous, she couldn't remain serious.

"Stop laughing, you don't need to overdo it," Saul said. "I may not look exactly like a movie heartthrob, but I can protect you against big, bad Jeffrey Langley for a few hours. If you wish, I'll engage him in a duel and make him pay dearly for whatever dastardly deed you think he is guilty of." Saul pretended to brandish a sword.

Carla laughed harder, her body shaking as she watched Saul perform a dueling dance with his imaginary enemy. "There, now," he said, standing beside her, "I've got you in a good mood again. Keep that poise and I'll pick you up at six. It'll give me a chance to see your townhouse and my cabinet."

"Your cabinet? After the price you charged for it, I feel it's definitely mine. It cost almost as much as the house."

"A slight exaggeration, but if I hadn't charged you a hefty price, you wouldn't have appreciated that wonderful piece of craftsmanship." He clasped her hands for a moment, released them, and went out the door. He turned toward her as he stood on the top step. "Tonight at six. Don't dress too formally, please. I'll be wearing this." He indicated his tweed jacket and flannel slacks. He turned and walked to his car. Carla was left standing in the middle of her office smiling at the empty air.

Dear, dear Saul, he always left her feeling better. She pictured the two of them sailing into Jeffrey's house arm in arm and laughed again.

CHAPTER 17

Carla wasn't in a jolly mood as she surveyed the contents of her closet trying to decide what to wear. She took down several dresses, considered some, but rejected them. Then her hand closed over a pale beige knitted sheath, sleeveless with a round neckline. It's matching long, shawl collar jacket with lacy diamond-patterned pointelle design hung on a separate hanger. She took dress and jacket from the closet and laid them over the wicker chair. She opened her jewelry box and found a double strand gold chain that complemented perfectly with her dress. She hunted through her shoe collection until she found the pale blond pumps.

Stripping off the clothes she had worn all day, Carla padded to the bathroom and stepped under the shower she had adjusted to wash away her fatigue. At one point, she had considered calling Saul and telling him she was too tired to go to the gathering at Jeffrey's house. But, she would have ended up doing exactly what she was doing now; preparing to go to dinner at the house of the man she had sworn never to see again. How long had it been since she had last seen Jeffrey — a month? It had seemed longer, like years. The picture of the last time she had seen him flashed through her mind. On the screen of her brain she saw Jeffrey and Sydney Allen playing out their roles. Sydney with her long blonde hair and eyes that matched her jade green silk dress. Carla recalled vividly the silent ride, sitting next to Jeffrey, from Secret Canyon Drive to Saguaro

Square. She still heard the sound of Jeffrey's truck as he drove away.   His words, "You're making a big mistake," lingered in her memory.

Carla thought of Jeffrey constantly and hated herself for doing so. Once in a while she was able to block him from her mind while she concentrated on her work. But he would creep back into her thoughts, crowding out everything else.

Now, standing under the shower, she lathered her tired body and rubbed the bubbles of soap into her weary pores.   She wondered how she would get through the evening. She watched the lather swirling around her feet.   As each bubble disappeared, she thought that was the way her relationship with Jeffrey had been going.   Slowly, bubble by bubble, it was washing away, down the drain of time until he would be a far away memory like the lingering perfume of the soap on her skin.

How will I face him tonight, she asked herself as she turned off the shower spray and stepped out onto the soft bathmat. What will I say to him? Small talk, yes, lots of small talk. The weather, my work, and I'll ask about his business trips. As she rubbed the drops of water from her firm, slender body still tanned from a long Tucson summer, she planned her conversation. Ask about Charlie and about the horses on the Rocking-L. Had he been out to the ranch lately?

She began to brush her hair with long, even strokes, coaxing it into sleek, shining waves around her shoulders.   The makeup she had planned went on slowly, with care. Just the right amount of blusher and lip gloss to offset the neutral color of the dress and shoes. Her reflection in the mirror satisfied her.

Carla went to the bedroom and eased on pale colored pantyhose. Then she slipped on a pale beige bra. She pulled the matching half slip over her legs, easing it to her hips and smoothing it in place. She pushed her toes into the blond pumps and took the dress from the padded hanger. She eased the dress over her head, pulled it down over her hips, and fastened the zipper in the back. She slipped the gold chain over her head, adjusting its double strands as she looked at her reflection in the mirror. She surveyed herself, turning from side to side and decided she would pass inspection.

It would have been better if she could have relaxed in a bubble bath for an hour, but there hadn't been time for such luxury. She thought of the large bathroom at the house on Secret Canyon Drive. She remembered sitting in the huge marble tub with Jeffrey and blushed. Why did she have to remember things like that? Why couldn't she forget him?

She turned to the wicker chair and picked up her jacket. Her small leather bag was lying on top of the chest of drawers in the bedroom. She put it over her arm and made her way down to the living room.

The doorbell sounded, and she hurried to the front door. She looked out through the peephole, it was Saul. She pulled the door open and stood aside as he came in.

"Hello, dear," he said, kissing her cheek. "You look lovely."

"Thank you. I thought you were going to wear the

same clothes you were wearing when you came to my office.

"Well, I got to thinking," Saul said. "Why not go all out for the occasion."

"You look very nice," Carla said. Saul was wearing a two piece suit in a dark blue. He looked very handsome with his gray hair, mustache, and full beard.

"Where is my beautiful cabinet? I want to see how you are treating it."

"Right this way." Carla led him across the living room to the wall where the antique cabinet stood. He put out his hand and touched the old wood lovingly. His deep voice cooed as though the cabinet were human. "Ooh, its lovely, isn't it?" he asked. "I wouldn't have sold it to any other person in the world."

"Unless someone else had the money to buy it," Carla smiled.

"No, honestly, only to you. There it was the first time I saw it, dusty, shabby in an old store in Mexico. I knew it needed a loving home with someone who would respect it, and immediately I thought of you."

Saul looked around the living room. "I like the way you've furnished this room. Very nice," Saul said. The simple country-look had transformed a contemporary townhouse into something quite different. Saul picked up an object here and there, examined it, and set it down again.

He looked at his watch. "Well, it's time to leave," he said. Carla picked up her knitted jacket and her purse which she had laid on a chair. Saul took her arm, "You're a lovely woman, Carla."

"Thank you, kind sir."

"Oh, it isn't idle praise. I say it after long study; comparing you to the many women I have known in a long lifetime. You are attractive and you deserve only the best."

They stood beside Saul's car. He opened the door and Carla got in. "I really don't know much about Jeffrey's social life, Carla. I wonder who else will be at the party."

"I have no idea," she said. "I'm afraid I don't know much about his social circle either."

"I thought you and he had become dear friends," Saul said as he got into the car and started the engine.

"No," Carla said. "And I really couldn't care less right now who his friends are."

Saul stole a look at her as he started to back the car out of the drive. "That has a false ring to it," he said. Carla shrugged her shoulders.

As they neared Jeffrey's house, Carla noticed that it was losing that new look. It was acquiring a more settled-in look, thanks to Frank and the wonderful job he was doing with the landscaping.

There were four—no—five cars in the parking area near the house. Lights were showing through the wide windows. Carla could see people moving about in the living room. This was more than a casual dinner. She was glad she had dressed appropriately.

She and Saul were met at the door by Frank Ebers. "Good evening, Carla. May I take your scarf and hat, sir?"

"Hello, Frank. It's good to see you. This is my friend, Saul Watkins. How's Alma?" Carla asked while Saul surrendered his silk scarf and soft wool fedora to Frank.

"It is a pleasure to meet you, sir, and Alma's fine." Frank hung the hat on a rack near the door. He took Carla's jacket and put it on a shelf. "She's busy in the kitchen helping the cook. We have a bigger staff now. Alma's now the housekeeper. She's glad she doesn't have so many responsibilities."

"That's good. It's a big house for only two people to do all the work when entertaining," Carla said. She and Saul moved toward the living room. In the archway between the living room and foyer they were met by Jeffrey.

"Saul, glad you could make it." He shook Saul's hand, and then turned to Carla. "What a nice surprise."

Carla met his gaze and couldn't decide whether to smile or frown. Jeffrey took her hands in his. "This is a pleasure. I didn't expect to see you, but, I hadn't given up entirely."

"Hello, Jeffrey," she said, deciding on a smile.

"While you two are catching up on old times, I'll go into the living room," Saul said. "I see someone I want to speak to." He moved past and left them standing in the archway, Jeffrey still imprisoning Carla's hands.

"How are you?" Jeffrey's voice was so low she had to turn her head to hear his words.

"I'm fine," she answered, smiling brightly. "My work has been taking up all my time leaving me exhausted."

"Thank God for hard work. Without it, I don't know how I'd have gotten through these past weeks. I've missed you very much." He was devouring her with his eyes, his gaze taking in all the details of her face as though he were filing them away for future reference.

She also looked at him, her fake smile, and brilliant remarks forgotten. She hadn't remembered he was so tanned, and had forgotten he was so tall. He looked tired, but it was probably only jet lag from his trips crisscrossing the country.

Jeffrey released her hands. "Come. I want you to meet the others. He put an arm around her waist and guided her into the room full of people. That was when Carla came face to face with Sydney Allen. She stopped. Jeffrey looked down at her and urged, "Come on, please."

The tall, willowy form, the shoulder-length blond hair swirling about her head and settling on Sydney's shoulders once again made Carla feel small and insignificant. Sydney's green eyes locked on Carla's. For a moment, Carla felt like turning around and running from the house. As she felt the pressure of Jeffrey's arm at her waist, she squared her shoulders, froze a smile into place, and said, "Hello."

"How nice of you to come," Sydney said. "We weren't expecting you, were we Jeffrey?"

"She came with Saul Watkins," Jeffrey said, still

holding Carla about the waist. "You know, the antique dealer from Nogales."

"Oh, yes. The jolly man with the amusing collection of bric-a-brac and secondhand furniture."

"Some of that jolly man's bric-a-brac and secondhand furniture cost me a fortune," Jeffrey said.

"Well, dear, you insisted on turning the whole decorating job over to a total stranger," as she glared at Carla. "It serves you right, Jeffrey. I offered to do the decorating for you, or have you forgotten?"

"I'm the stranger who did the decorating," Carla snapped, "and Saul Watkins is very ethical. He's a well known and respected antiques dealer throughout the country."

"Oh, I hope I haven't offended anyone," Sydney said. "I realize that Mexican primitives are very well known, in some circles, at least."

"Sydney, I believe you can leave it right there. You're getting in a bit too deep, as usual. As for not wanting to offend, you're doing a pretty poor job of it. So, would you please back off?" Jeffrey's voice was icy.

Sydney looked into Jeffrey's eyes, her voice cool and even. "Thank you for the scolding, darling. I've been naughty, haven't I?" She turned to Carla. "Of course, Mexican primitives are very much at home in this area, aren't they? They're very amusing. I probably should get used to them, shouldn't I."

Jeffrey excused himself to greet another guest. Carla wished he had not left her alone with Sydney. She felt like she was under a microscope.

"It's an amusing house," Sydney continued. "I

particularly like the master bedroom, and the master bathroom is marvelous. What a pity the two rooms have to be redone. Jeffrey should have consulted me before he turned things over to you. The colors are wrong for me."

Ouch, Carla flinched. Your arrow hit its mark, lady. I know when I've been shot down. Carla looked at the tall blond. Her silk dress of periwinkle blue caressed her lithe body, stopping just below the knees. Her high-heeled matching sandals gave her the advantage of almost three additional inches. Carla felt very small. The beige knit costume she was wearing did nothing to increase her confidence.

"Yes," Carla said. "The color scheme would be wrong for you."

"I don't know if we should keep this house," Sydney told her. "I'm not sure I want to live in Tucson. Actually, our lives are centered on things in St. Louis and New York. I know one thing, I don't want to spend much time at that horrible ranch east of here — all cactus and rocks." She shuddered.

Suddenly Sydney said, "Pardon me. I want to talk to someone before she gets away." She turned to leave, then stopped, and turned back to Carla. "An amusing idea came to me. Perhaps I should have you redo the house. That is, in case I decide to stay here. I'm sure Jeffrey wouldn't mind if you did the whole thing over. He does whatever I want him to do." She had shot another arrow from her bow and it had found its mark. She turned away and moved across the room to a cluster of guests.

Sydney's meaning was quite clear. Carla had lost Jeffrey. Correction, you can't lose someone you never had.

Jeffrey came over to her.

"I didn't know Sydney was still here," Carla told him, "or, rather, that she had come back to Tucson. If I had known she was going to be here tonight, I would have stayed away," she mumbled. "I didn't want to come, but Saul insisted. I shouldn't have let him talk me into it."

"Sydney went back to New York, and then she returned to Tucson the day before yesterday."

"And camped out in the master suite?" Carla asked.

"No. I'm camped out in the master suite. That is, for tonight. I've been staying at the ranch lately."

"Your camping arrangements are really no concern of mine. You can put your bedroll any place you like," Carla retorted.

Jeffrey's hand clamped her arm. "Of course it's your concern."

"I have no right to question you, Jeffrey. It was rude of me."

"You have every right."

Carla lifted her eyes to his. "I—I don't have any—any —." She couldn't finish the sentence with him looking at her. She turned her head away. "I'm not interested in what you and Sydney Allen do."

His hold on her arm tightened. She could feel his breath against her face as he leaned toward her. The pounding of her heart was deafening her.

"Please, Carla," Jeffrey said. "Oh, Carla, what's

happening to us?"

She was spared having to answer that as another couple arrived. Frank Ebers had come into the room, escorting the new arrivals through the archway. Jeffrey turned to greet them and Carla took advantage of the interruption to slip away. She melted into the group assembled in the living room, taking a drink from a tray passed by a uniformed maid. As Carla lifted her glass to sip the chilled liquid, she saw Sydney standing across the room watching her.

It was a large group that assembled around the long table in the dining room. Carla counted fourteen people including herself. Jeffrey sat at the head of the table and Sydney at the foot. No matter how much Jeffrey might protest, he couldn't change the fact that Sydney had taken over the role of hostess.

Carla managed to get through the meal. She engaged in light conversation with people on either side of her. The dinner lasted nearly two hours — she was glad when it was over. She wanted to escape, to run out the front door and never stop running until she reached her little townhouse on Prince. But that was not something she was able to do. She had to finish this and look as if she were having a marvelous time. She would give neither Sydney nor Jeffrey the satisfaction of knowing how hurt she was. She would not let them know how Jeffrey had dashed her hopes for the future, even though he had sworn Sydney was only a friend and business acquaintance.

At last, dinner was over. The last spoonful of luscious dessert had been consumed. The last sips of coffee and wine had been consumed. When Saul finally signaled her that it was time to leave, she stood at the front door holding her hand out to Jeffrey and said goodnight. The pressure of his fingers on hers, the nearness of him, his breath fanning her face, was almost more than she could bear. She longed to press her body against his, to run her fingers through his hair, kiss those firm lips that were saying meaningless words although his eyes were sending a different message.

While Carla was saying goodnight, Sydney came over and slipped her arm through Jeffrey's. "Goodnight, Miss Meade—uhh, Carla," she said. "Think about my suggestion of possibly redoing the house in my favorite colors. It might be fun."

Carla remembered her first meeting with Sydney in this same doorway. It had been the day she returned from her first visit to the ranch. Men were all alike, really. She had thought Jeffrey was different, but he wasn't. He was like Peter. Peter had filled her with dreams and promises, and then taken them away, leaving a void in their place. Jeffrey had led her to believe he cared for her when Sydney had really been the woman in his life.

Sydney's voice rang in Carla's ears long after she and Saul had left the house and gotten into his car. "Fun," Sydney had said. Fun would be tightening her fingers around Sydney's hair and tugging very hard.

But that would put her in the same category with Sydney. She wasn't about to do that.

How Jeffrey could have let this woman take over his life, Carla didn't understand. Sydney had control and was carefully redoing him according to her plans. He would become a part of her background, like the house on Secret Canyon Drive. Jeffrey had even had the nerve to suggest that he and Carla could continue as before, as though Sydney were not a part of his life. Goodbye, Mr. Jeffrey G. Langley, she thought. If it were not over before, it was certainly over now.

Carla sat back against the bucket seat and looked out into the chill November night. Saul drove in silence.

Carla went to her bedroom dragging her feet. The evening had lasted interminably. She had felt a surge of relief when she had reached her townhouse and had said goodnight to Saul. When would she be able to erase from her mind the sight of Sydney with her arm entwined through Jeffrey's?

How I ever thought I could live in that house, she asked herself as she removed her jacket and put it on a padded hanger. Sydney's ghost will always walk around in that house. Even if she was to go away and Jeffrey and I were to get together, I could never be comfortable there.

She unzipped her dress and let it drop to the floor.

That was the house I dreamed of as mine when I was decorating it. Every object in it was placed as though it were mine, as though I would touch it and enjoy it day after day. And when I saw Jeffrey that first time, when I felt him near me, touching me, I wanted even more to live in that house — with him. Well, the dream is over, she resolved. I wish I could be rid of it. I wish I could wash it out of my brain and never think of him or his blasted house again.

Carla bent down to retrieve her dress from the floor. As she put it on a hanger and hung it in the closet, she remembered the times she had stood near Jeffrey and felt the currents of electricity pass between them. A weakness passed over her as she realized she would never feel that again. Don't remember, Carla, she said to herself. Don't put yourself through that exercise in futility. Put him out of your mind and concentrate on your work. You have to finish up the adobe house downtown. The grand opening is coming up soon. You are almost finished with that job, so concentrate on the finishing touches. There will be other decorating jobs. Something else will come along, it always does.

She felt chilled and found a long flannel granny gown and pulled it over her head. The folds of cloth wrapping themselves around her legs restored a feeling of warmth to her body. She was sitting on the side of the bed, ready to swing her legs up and tuck herself between the covers when the phone rang.

She glanced at the clock beside the telephone, nearly midnight. Who would be calling at this time of night? She reached out her hand to lift the phone to her ear and whispered, "Hello?"

"Carla?"

Oh, no, not Jeffrey. She couldn't bear to go through this. Hang up. How can you talk to him? He was so far away even though he was only on the other side of town. He might as well be in another world.

"Jeffrey, what do you want?" She breathed deeply.

"I want to discuss us, Carla, you and me. When I saw you tonight, I suddenly wanted to tell everybody to go home. I wanted to touch you, hold you, drag you into my bedroom, and make love to you."

"With Sydney there in the house?"

"Yes, and I still want to."

"You shouldn't be talking to me like this."

"Why not?"

Clara was silent. What kind of man is he? If he and Sydney were a twosome, then he was certainly being insensitive to her and her feelings and the conflict with Sydney there.

"What would you do if I were to come over to your house? Like right now? Would you let me in?" Jeffrey asked.

"No, I would not let you in."

"But you want to. You would want to let me in. I know it. Every time our eyes meet, every time I'm near you, I feel that you want to be alone with me as I do with you. Oh, Carla, I want you so. I'm going to jump in the truck and come over there. Right now."

"No! No, Jeffrey, you are not going to come over here. Go to bed and go to sleep. You have a houseguest and the proper host doesn't go off in the night leaving his guest alone in the house. Remember your manners, Jeffrey. Good night!" She said icily. With a little smile that quickly turned into a frown, Carla put the phone on the bedside table and climbed into bed. She turned on her side and closed her eyes thinking about his call.

"Don't remember, Carla," she told herself. "Don't do this to yourself. Put him out of your mind. Concentrate on your work. It has always helped before. It can do the trick again. There's the old adobe house in old Tucson to finish. You're almost through there. And other clients will have decorating jobs around Tucson for you. And, when they're finished, something else will come along. It always has."

Suddenly she felt herself shivering. She was glad she was wearing her old granny gown.

CHAPTER 18

Sleep refused to come. As night was turning into day, Carla finally fell asleep. The shattering shrieks from the alarm clock brought her to a sitting position, wondering where she was and what had happened. She reached out to shut off the offending alarm. Rubbing her eyes that refused to focus on such short notice, she felt stiff and sore. Her mind was blurred. She shook her head, trying to get the brain cells to function normally.

Forcing herself to move to the side of the bed and stand up, she thought back to the night before. No wonder she felt tired. Yesterday evening had been a disaster that she would never want to repeat. She stood and wandered into the bathroom, bumping her thigh against the door frame. She stripped off the flannel gown and let it drop to the floor. She turned on the shower, adjusted the water to a comfortable temperature, and stepped inside. The shower performed miracles, as it had done many times before. Her weariness was leaving her. After a long time under the hot, invigorating spray, she stepped out and toweled dry. She looked at herself in the long mirror. It had only been yesterday that she had gone to Jeffrey's house for dinner. Last night was still vivid in her mind. She thought of Jeffrey and realized she may have driven him away.

She still wanted him so very much. But he was not hers. Sydney had made that clear. "I'll put him out of my mind," she said to herself. "I have other things to do."

As she hung the damp towel over a bar and put her nightgown on the hook on the back of the door, Carla went to the bedroom. She tried to organize her thoughts. She would go to the office after breakfast. There was a stack of mail to be answered. That was step number one. Step number two was to go to the restoration project in the historic district. The little adobe house would need several hours of her attention. There was still a lot to be done before the opening in two weeks. It was difficult to realize that November was almost over.

Carla opened the closet door and took out a teal and camel plaid skirt. After brushing her hair and applying makeup, she put on the coordinating teal sweater and went to the kitchen. Breakfast was her usual orange juice, coffee and buttered toast. It didn't take Carla long to prepare and consume breakfast while sitting on a stool at the counter.

The drive to her office on Ft. Lowell Road took the usual amount of time. The street was a heavily traveled artery across town. That was the reason Carla, along with many others, had chosen it as a place for her business. There were always lots of opportunities for drivers to glance at the shops along their way. When she reached her shop, she parked in the parking area, locked the car, and went to her office. Unlocking the door, she went inside, touching her display pieces of furniture, and vases and figurines arranged on the wall shelves.

She sat down and pulled a stack of mail and printouts toward her and began to read. When she had reviewed everything, she arranged the literature into different piles by vendor or client. She worked for an hour, organized her desk, picked up her tote bag, and left the shop, locking the door behind her. She went to her car, unlocked the door on the driver's side, and got in. Soon she was part of the stream of traffic headed toward downtown Tucson.

Carla spent the rest of the day at the old adobe house. Professor Cantrell came in after lunch. "Good news," he said as he put a brochure in front of her where she was sitting at the old wooden table. On the front of the brochure was a full color photo of the adobe house. Beneath it was the message: "Grand Opening of the Ramirez House." The date of the opening was the Saturday before Thanksgiving.

Old Adobe Ramirez House in Tucson

"Oh, that's wonderful," Carla said.

"Yes, all your hard work will be appreciated when people file through here and see this place looking the way it did years ago when it was new," the professor said.

"I love this house," Carla said. "It has been fun to work on and make it look new again."

"But not too new, that was the clever part. It looks like people still live here, that daily life still goes on. It doesn't look like a museum."

Knowing that admittance to the celebration was by invitation only, Carla asked, "Will I be invited to the Grand Opening?"

"Of course, and here's your invitation." He pulled an ivory colored envelope from his brief case. Her name was handwritten across the front. Carla opened the envelope and pulled out the engraved invitation. "Oh, I'm thrilled to be included. Taking this adobe through its restoration has meant a lot to me."

"There will be lots of celebrities. Even some important people from Mexico. The Mayor of Tucson will be here and the District Representative to Congress, Francisco Ramirez, with his family. It's going to be a great occasion."

"Could I bring a guest?" Carla asked. She thought Marge would like to see this.

"Yes, of course." The professor pulled another invitation out of his briefcase.

After Professor Cantrell left, Carla spent an hour checking the house to see that everything was in order. It was a thrill to know that her restoration skills would be on display. Marge's eyes would pop when she saw the detail of Carla's work.

Carla stayed at the adobe house for about an hour, then closed the heavy front door, and locked it as she left. Putting the key in her handbag, she walked briskly along the sidewalk to her car which was parked down the street. The cool air added to the exhilaration she felt at being able to show her latest decorating accomplishment.

CHAPTER 19

Carla woke up early that Saturday before Thanksgiving. She got out of bed, went to the bathroom, and pulled off her flannel gown. She showered and shampooed her hair.

After drying off with a fluffy towel, she combed her still wet hair. She would let it dry, and then comb it again. The curls and waves would arrange themselves. There was no point in trying to set her hair into a particular fashion. She had learned early in life that it would do its own thing.

Today is the big day, she said to the sky as she opened the blinds in the bedroom. She straightened the sheets and the quilt on her bed and plumped up the pillows. Marge had made the yellow quilt. She passed her hand over it, once again admiring the tiny stitches that held it together.

Marge was going with her to the opening of the Ramirez House. The old adobe house in downtown Tucson had been restored and refurnished at last with the most beautiful things Carla had ever seen. Thanks to Saul, she had a wonderful supply of antiques to display.

After a breakfast of coffee, orange juice and buttered twelve-grain bread, Carla picked up her briefcase and drove to her office on Ft. Lowell Road. The sign in front always pleased her. It advertised to the world what she had become through hard work and perseverance.

The new sign had arrived last week. Carla had

stood in the sun watching as the workmen installed it over the door of her shop.

DESIGN FOR YOU

Interior Decorating

Old Spain and Early Arizona

She now unlocked the door and walked inside. Going to her desk, she put down her briefcase. She opened her Weekly Planner and began reviewing her notes. After a few minutes, she went to the door and stooped to pick up her mail. There was a lot of it. She took it to her desk and began to sort the envelopes, magazines and assorted pamphlets. There were mostly advertisements and a few bills. Oh, here was something interesting. She put this handwritten envelope to one side to look at later.

The morning was spent on phone calls, reading her mail, and reviewing her messages. When lunchtime came, Carla went to the small refrigerator and pulled out a soda. She looked in a little cupboard near the refrigerator and found a box of whole wheat crackers. She drank the soda and munched on the crackers as she walked around her studio, admiring the beautiful pieces of furniture and the accessories that filled the large room.

Back at her desk, she worked until two o'clock. Then she grabbed her briefcase and handbag, and left the office. There was not much traffic at this time of the afternoon. She passed El Hombre. Tony had apparently gone home since his pickup and kitchen trailer were not there. When Carla arrived at her townhouse, she parked in the carport and went to her front door. Unlocking the door, she walked into the living room.

Whew, she sighed, I worked longer than I thought. She put her briefcase and handbag on a table and stretched out on the sofa. It didn't take very long to fall sleep.

The sound of the telephone ringing awakened Carla. She hurried to the phone and picked it up. "Yes? Oh, hi Marge."

"You sound like you just woke up," Marge's voice filled her ears.

"You guessed it. I worked hard this morning and just conked out on the sofa when I got home. What time is it?" Carla looked at the clock on the wall in front of her. "Oh, my heavens, it's that late?"

"It's five o'clock. The big occasion starts at seven. You'd better get busy. You've got to change into a popular young interior decorator."

"Thanks for calling, Marge. I would have slept through and missed the whole thing."

"Get going, gal. I'm going to start transforming myself into something more exotic in just a minute or two. When should I come over?"

"I'll be ready about six," Carla stated.

"Oh, good. We can be there by six-thirty then, which will give you plenty of time to double-check everything before the guests start arriving. 'Bye." Carla put down the phone and went to the bedroom to get ready.

A quick shower under the spray of hot water cleared her mind of all that had taken place during the day and prepared herself for the evening to come. She had worked long and hard to bring the old, forsaken adobe house on the edge of what had been a barrio into the beautiful place it was now. In decorating the house, every care had been taken to make it authentic. It had become a perfect reflection of the mode of furnishing and decorating at the time when it was built. Tonight, others would see the results of her labors. They would never know all the details, the planning, and the work that went into what they were seeing. Saul's efforts and the labor of many others, as well as her long hours would finally be realized.

After she showered and dried herself, Carla went to the vanity and carefully applied her makeup and brushed her hair into place.

Standing in front of her closet in her beige bra and panties and a matching half slip, Carla slipped her feet into gold high-heeled pumps and took her favorite beige silk dress off its hanger. Pulling the dress over her head and smoothing it as it slipped over her body, she started to relax. A matching beige silk jacket completed her costume. She put it on, found her beige evening bag with gold sequins, and went through the bedroom to the living room.

The doorbell was sounding at the front door. Carla strode to open the door. "Let me in," Marge said, "it's chilly out here." Carla stood aside and Marge entered. Marge was wearing a royal blue silk pant suit. Her high-heeled sandals were black. She carried a silver colored silk bag. Her dark hair had been swept to the top of her head in curls.

"Marge, you look great," Carla said.

"I didn't want you to be ashamed of me," Marge said, patting her hair.

"Ashamed? Hardly, let's get underway," Carla said.

The two women went outside. Carla pulled the door shut and checked to see that it was locked. They went to Carla's Honda and got in. The drive through east Tucson in the early evening was pleasant. They followed Broadway downtown. When they reached the adobe house, cars were parked on both sides of the street leaving a cleared space in front of the house for valet parking. An attendant wearing an identifying badge helped them get out of the car, and then drove the aging Civic to a parking area.

Carla and Marge walked up to the front door of the adobe house. Another attendant asked for their invitations, which Carla and Marge produced. When they had been checked against the guest list, the attendant opened the door and they entered the house. It was full of people milling about as easily as possible. It was a not that large a house.

Carla saw Saul across the room. He was talking to two men and a woman. Saul noticed Carla and Marge and waved to them. As they started across the room to say hello, Carla saw Jeffrey. He saw her and smiled. The woman beside him turned. It was Sydney.

"I'm ready to go home," Carla whispered to Marge.

"You're what?"

"Never mind. Just someone here I'd rather not see. Come on, let's get this over with." She started moving in the direction of Jeffrey and Sydney.

"Mr. Langley, how nice to see you."

Jeffrey took her hand. Sydney looked at her. Jeffrey said, "Good to see you, Carla. And who is this lovely lady?" as he turned to Marge.

"May I present Marge Jenkins, my friend and next door neighbor?"

"Oh, yes," Marge said. "The man whose house you decorated. How do you do."

As Sydney turned toward them, Jeffrey said, "And this is Sydney Allen. She is visiting me for a few days."

Sydney — tall and elegant in a long turquoise dress, a long gold chain around her neck, and turquoise satin sandals peeking from beneath the hem of her dress — turned and extended her hand to Marge. "I'm pleased to meet you. It was so nice of both of you to come this evening. We do hope you will have a lovely time. You'll never know how much time, effort, and money Jeffrey has put into this place. Do look around and enjoy yourselves. Now, if you'll excuse us, I see we have other guests." She pointed to a group that had just entered.

"Sydney, please!" Jeffrey said sternly.

"Oh, never mind, Jeffrey," Carla said. "Nice seeing

you." She moved away and Marge followed.

"Who was that?" Marge asked.

"That was the woman I was telling you about. She's trying to take over Jeffrey's house, his life, everything."

"A little of her can go a long way," Marge retorted.

They met Saul in the dining room. "Carla, it's great to see you."

"Saul, this is my friend and next door neighbor, Marge Jenkins. Marge, Saul Watkins."

"How nice to meet you, Ms. Jenkins."

"Marge is the quilter I told you about, Saul. She makes handbags and totes as well as quilts. All hand sewn and excellent quality."

"Ah, yes. We'll have to get together soon. I might be interested in your quilts. I don't deal in them, but they could be a nice addition to my shop. Do you have a card?"

Marge opened her bag and pulled out a small bundle of business cards. She extracted one of them and gave it to Saul. "I never leave home without them."

"Smart girl and here is one of mine," Saul said. "I'll be in touch." They smiled at each other.

"Now, if you'll excuse us," Carla said, "we'll move on and let the rest of your adoring public have a chance."

The two women went to the refreshment table and were served by a pretty young woman in a Mexican costume. As they walked about in the crowded room, sipping their drink and nibbling hors d'oeuvres, Carla was pleased at the crowd that had gathered.

"There really is no way you can appreciate this

house tonight. There are far too many people," Carla told Marge.

Just then a voice said, "Ladies and Gentlemen, may I have your attention?" The noise in the room stilled and Professor Edward Cantrell continued, "This is a very special evening. We are here to add this magnificent house to our impressive list of architectural delights in the city of Tucson. Because of the hard work of many people in many lines of expertise — not to mention the generous monetary contributions, for which we are most grateful — we are able to present this house to you tonight." Applause filled the room.

Professor Cantrell introduced the man who had started the project; a woman, a member of the family who had once lived in the house; and Jeffrey Langley, whose personal funding had made the restoration possible. He then turned to Carla and said, "And now, the person who oversaw the restoration of the interior of the Ramirez House, Miss Carla Meade, the owner of Design for You. Miss Meade —."

Carla stepped forward and bowed to the people in the room. The applause reaching her ears made her smile. I believe they appreciate what they have seen, she thought. Soon after, Carla and Marge said their goodbyes and retreated to leave. As she and Marge neared the exit, Jeffrey came over to her. Sydney followed him.

"You did a great job, Carla," Jeffrey said.

"Thank you," she said.

"Your expertise really shows."

Sydney smugly said, "Well, darling, anybody could

make a dump like this look better with just a coat of paint. I hate these old piles of rock. This place should have been torn down and something decent built here."

"Sydney," Jeffrey said. "Be quiet! That's an order. This house isn't made of rocks; it's made of adobe and is an historic landmark."

"Well, whatever," Sydney responded as she turned and walked away.

Carla and Marge shook their heads as they smiled at Sydney and left the house. They recovered the Honda and Carla drove home through the November evening.

CHAPTER 20

Thanksgiving Day arrived with sunshine, moderate temperatures and an occasional gust of wind—just enough to need an anchor for the tablecloth. Carla was going to celebrate Thanksgiving on the patio with her friends. Carla had spent Wednesday cleaning the patio. She had weeded the plant containers, hosed down the tiles of the patio floor, and eliminated as many cobwebs as she could reach. After a quick vacuuming and dusting of the living room and bedroom, a thorough cleaning of the bathroom and the kitchen, Carla pronounced the house and patio ready for visitors.

Marge, Anna, and Pearl with her eight year old son, Billy, were coming. The girls were bringing the main dishes for Thanksgiving dinner. Carla had been assigned to make the salad. She had told them she would provide the wine and after-dinner coffee.

Beginning to prepare the salad, she put fresh lettuce leaves on each plate and piled a generous serving of cottage cheese topped with fresh fruit on top of the lettuce. Then she put a dollop of mayonnaise on each salad. When Carla had finished, she looked at the clock over the counter. Just enough time to shower and dress for the big event. She hugged herself. She loved parties. She loved Thanksgiving.

Carla finished showering and dressing just in time. Her makeup had given her a little trouble. She had applied eyeliner and taken it off twice before it turned out right. She was giving her hair a final brushing when the doorbell sounded. Putting the brush on the vanity, she hurried out of the bathroom, through the bedroom to the front door. Marge stood on the front stoop.

"Hi, am I too early?" She held a roasting pan in her hands.

"No, come in, Marge," Carla said. "Go to the kitchen and put that roaster down. We don't want you to drop the turkey."

"It certainly would make a mess on your living room carpet if I did," Marge replied.

"Never mind the carpet. We'd lose the turkey and I'm hungry!" Carla laughed. "I got off easy this time. Just had to provide a salad."

"But you're providing your house and patio," Marge said. "We have to have someplace to eat. And our having Thanksgiving dinner on the patio was a great idea."

"Glad to be of service, ma'am." Carla bowed. "I hope it won't be too cool. The weather is certainly changing."

"Oh, I think it'll be warm enough on the patio. It's sheltered and the sun is out today," Marge said as she put the roaster with the turkey on the counter.

"I was just going to set the table now," Carla said following her.

"I'll help," Marge said. "Placemats or tablecloth?"

"What do you think?"

"I think placemats. That way, we can be messy if we want. Whatever spills on the floor, we just hose off after we've finished eating," Marge said.

"Placemats it is." Carla went to the buffet, opened a drawer, and took out gold, brown, rust, and dark green striped placemats. She found the matching napkins and carried them to the patio, setting them around the table. From the top of the buffet in the dining area, she took a bouquet of chrysanthemums in a low vase and put it in the center of the patio table. Standing off to one side, she looked at the scene before her and said, "There."

"It looks beautiful," Marge said.

The doorbell sounded again. Carla went inside, walked to the front door, and opened it. Pearl and Billy stood there. Pearl was holding a large bowl covered with a kitchen towel. Billy also held a covered bowl.

"Come in; come in," Carla said, "Happy Thanksgiving!"

"Here are the potatoes and the broccoli, and same to you," Pearl said.

"I've got the broccoli," Billy said.

"Straight through to the kitchen, madam and sir," Carla said, bowing and extending her arm.

Billy giggled as he and his mother came inside. They went to the kitchen. Carla could hear Pearl talking to Marge. Billy came back to the living room.

"Well, Billy, how are things going?"

"Okay, I guess."

"School's all right?"

"Yeah."

"Working hard?"

"Yeah."

"Do you want to watch TV? There's going to be a football game that's starting soon."

"Yeah, I guess so." Billy went to the TV and turned it on. He found the proper channel, plopped down on the floor to watch the screen.

Carla went to the kitchen and was starting to help Marge and Pearl when the doorbell rang again. She hurried back through the dining area and living room to the front door. She opened the door.

Anna, holding a large serving bowl, covered with a plastic dome, said, "Hi, Happy Thanksgiving. This is heavy."

"Take it straight through to the kitchen, Anna," Carla said.

About thirty minutes later the four women had put the dinner together and called Billy. They went out to the patio; Billy followed reluctantly as he looked back at the TV screen. The table was laden with food. They sat down to begin their Thanksgiving feast. After Carla said grace, they began to eat their salads. Carla sipped her wine, took a bite of salad, and looked around the table. Good friends sharing good food. It was a wonderful Thanksgiving.

The dining lasted over an hour. Billy kept running back and forth, watching the football game, and eating dinner at the same time. The women's conversation centered on their work, their other friends and acquaintances, the weather, and their jobs.

"How's it going with Jeffrey?" Anna asked Carla.

"He was at the opening of the adobe house the other night," Marge said.

"I know," Anna said. "I saw it in the paper."

"I talked to him, of course," Carla said, "but only for

a few minutes. There were a lot of people and speeches, too."

"His girlfriend was with him," Marge said.

"Oh?" Pearl said. "I thought —."

"Yeah, that's what I thought, too. But I guess I was wrong."

"You didn't tell us he has a girlfriend," Anna said to Carla.

"Let's just leave it. I don't want to discuss the matter right now." Carla picked up her wine glass and took a sip.

"Well, I guess that takes care of that," Pearl said.

"How is your business going, Marge?" Anna asked.

The conversation turned to Marge's enterprise. Carla sat there turning her wine glass around and around.

When the conversation between the other women stopped, Billy said, "Mom, you promised me that we could leave after dinner and we're through eating." He had taken a last bite of the wedge of pumpkin pie before him. "I'm through now."

"Billy, be polite. Sorry gals, I did promise Billy. He has a date with his friends."

The women got up from the table and followed Billy to the other end of the living room. After a few minutes of conversation, Pearl and Billy left.

"Children do demand attention, don't you think?" Anna asked as she, Carla, and Marge cleared the table and carried the used dishes to the kitchen.

"We were probably that way too, when we were that age," Carla said. "It's part of being young. They have things on their minds, I guess."

"By the way, where is your Jeffrey?" Anna asked.

"Yes," said Marge, "I expected him to at least call you."

"He's probably in St. Louis," Carla said. "He's an important man, you know. He's probably having dinner somewhere, with friends or relatives, or entertaining at his place."

"Does he have a house? Or, an apartment? Maybe a condo?" Anna asked.

Carla said, "In St. Louis? I don't know. We've never discussed it. I only know that he has the house on Secret Canyon Drive here in Tucson and the ranch at Texas Canyon near Dragoon."

"You sure don't know too much about that guy," Marge said.

"No, I guess I don't," Carla said.

The women had finished clearing away the remains of the feast and Anna was rinsing the dishes and glassware and stacking them into the dishwasher. "What I don't like is his being so cozy with you and having that other woman too," she said.

"Now, let's be fair," Carla said. "I don't know for sure what his relationship is with Sydney. They may be just business partners, as he said."

"Some business, if you ask me," Marge said.

"Ladies, let's get on with clearing the dishes and then have a nice game of three-handed rummy on the patio," said Carla as she started to clean the counter.

CHAPTER 21

The sun was shining in Carla's eyes as she turned to her right side. She welcomed the warm quilt that had kept her cozy during the night. She got out of bed and stretched as she had decided to make today a work day. There was plenty that waited for her at the office. The answering machine might have collected messages over the holiday, and she remembered there was a pile of unopened envelopes on her desk.

After a shower and the usual battle with her hair, she put on makeup and went through the familiar routine of selecting clothes; blue jeans and a sweater. She found her favorite jeans on a hanger in the closet. Ah, and that pink sweater hadn't been worn since last spring. She carried the clothes to her bed, found a bra, panties, and socks in the chest of drawers, and began to dress. She pushed her feet into moccasins.

Yesterday had been fun. She always enjoyed her time with Marge, Pearl, and Anna. Overall, Billy had been a young gentleman. He didn't have a very large vocabulary, but she remembered when she was in third grade. What a bore it had been when there was no one to play with, being stuck with a bunch of adults.

She went into the kitchen and prepared her usual breakfast of toast, orange juice, and coffee. There was a left-over piece of pumpkin pie. She decided she would eat that when she poured her second cup of coffee.

When the coffee and toast were ready, she sat on the high stool at the counter and thought about her work.

Decorating the adobe house had been her last assignment. Now she was free for awhile. It had been a long time since she had no work waiting in the wings. Until after Christmas, work would be slow. She thought of the things she could do to use up the time until jobs started coming in.

The winter visitors would keep her busy until spring. Tucson real estate sales were always good during the winter. The new homeowners would want their homes decorated. And there were always redecorating jobs. People grew tired of their living room furniture, or wanted to turn a bedroom into a den or office — or, wanted to repaint the interior and didn't know what kind of paint or color, and surely didn't want to do the work themselves. Carla looked at the clock. It was time to head for the office. She put her dishes in the sink and went to the bedroom to get her handbag. Her briefcase was lying on the dining room table. She picked it up as she passed the table and left the house, locking the front door behind her.

She glanced at Marge's house as she went to her carport. The blinds had been opened in the front window. Marge was probably already hard at work in the back corner of her dining room. She had turned the dining area into a workshop where she designed and turned out her handmade quilts.

Carla got into her car and drove down the lane, crossing the three speed bumps and turned out of Saguaro Square onto Prince Road. When she reached Ft. Lowell, she passed El Hombre. Tony's kitchen trailer was not there. No cars were parked in the lot.

Nobody was lined up, waiting to order breakfast. The tables and chairs were packed away in the storage building. The El Hombre restaurant would not reopen until March. Tony would be working at one of the tourist hotels until spring.

When Carla reached her shop, she parked in the parking area, got out of the Honda, and unlocked the door, looking up at the sign. It was always a thrill to walk into her own shop. She acknowledged she had worked long and hard to get to this place. It was quite an accomplishment to have a shop on Ft. Lowell Road.

Entering the front room, she turned on the lights. As she went to her office in the corner, she scanned the accessories arranged on the shelves and display tables along the side of the room. The desk was neat except for a stack of envelopes on one side. She sat down and put her handbag in a drawer and her briefcase on the floor next to the desk. She pressed Replay on the answering machine and began to check her messages. There were no messages from Jeffrey. She thought she had carefully put him out of her mind during the Thanksgiving break. Now she started thinking about him again. Where had he spent Thanksgiving Day? Was he in St. Louis, at the ranch in Texas Canyon, or at his place here in Tucson? Was he alone or with Sydney? Carla wondered if she would ever see him again.

She started opening envelopes. When she had opened all the mail and arranged the contents by date and subject matter, she looked at the clock. Time for lunch already. She went to a cabinet over the little counter where she made coffee. Whole grain crackers. She took down the cracker box and opened the small refrigerator under the counter, taking out a container of milk. She also reached for an apple. Picking up a paper napkin from the counter, she carried the milk, crackers, and apple to her desk. She opened a drawer and sat down, propping her feet on the edge of the drawer and began to eat.

Noticing a letter on top of the stack of mail, she pulled it forward. It was written by hand. She opened the envelope and looked at the names at the bottom of the page, Catherine and Frank Duncan. Carla read the letter carefully. The handwriting was easy to read. Mr. and Mrs. Duncan had purchased an old adobe house in San Isidro, New Mexico. They wanted to have it restored. Carla beamed when she read they wanted her to handle the restoration and decorate it authentically when the restoration was finished. They had been guests at the opening ceremonies of the Ramirez House in downtown Tucson. The Duncans were impressed when they viewed the restoration and learned at the ceremony that she was the decorator. They wanted her to authentically redecorate their adobe house. The telephone number of the Duncans was at the top of the page with their address. Carla dialed the number. After a short wait, a woman's voice answered, "Hello?"

"Mrs. Duncan?" Carla asked.

"Yes."

"I'm Carla Meade, interior decorator and owner of Design for You. I have just finished reading your letter."

"Oh, wonderful," Mrs. Duncan said. "Then you know that my husband, Frank, and I have purchased an old house in a little town in New Mexico. We want you to oversee the restoration and to decorate it according to the period when the house was originally built."

"Do you realize, Mrs. Duncan, that you may need some modern conveniences, like indoor bathrooms, kitchen upgrades, or a laundry room? And then there is the electricity, city utilities of course, as well as heating, air conditioning, modern plumbing, etc., as a part of the restoration … that is, if you're planning to live in it?"

"Oh, yes, of course," Mrs. Duncan said. "But that's why we chose you for the job. You'll know how to properly disguise those upgrades and not let them dominate the old house. Oh, please, tell me you'll take the job. We so much want your involvement in it."

"I'd like to look at the house first. I can go there and look at it in December and give you my answer. I can't do very much interior decorating before the restoration is finished, and that's not likely to happen before spring, of course. I assume the weather would make restoration almost impossible."

"That would be all right. We just want your answer. The reconstruction of the house hasn't been finished yet. The contractor told me he would have to stop at the end of this month and wait until spring to finish."

"Then that will give me plenty of time to look the house over and make my plans for decorating," Carla said. "I will let you know by the fifteenth of January."

"Oh, thank you, Miss Meade."

"I'll send you a letter of confirmation."

"We'll be waiting for it."

"Very well, Mrs. Duncan. Goodbye."

"Goodbye, Miss Meade."

Carla heard the click. San Isidro—to do an old house on a narrow, rutted street in a tiny town high in the mountains of New Mexico.

"Well, how about that," she thought as she pushed the letter away from herself. "I had never thought I would go back to San Isidro." She sat back at her desk in astonishment at the invitation to return to her home town after leaving so long ago. "Can I possibly take that job?" she wondered to herself.

Carla reached out and pulled a tissue from the box on her desk as memories returned. She wiped her eyes and blew her nose. "What an opportunity. And this job will expand my portfolio. I can get help from Saul. He'll know a lot about the history of the area. He'll be able to provide more antiques from the period of the house. I can almost see it now." Carla got up from her desk and walked around the office. There was a carved image of a saint on a little shelf along the wall. She picked it up, looked at it, and put it back. She was trying to imagine how the house would be redecorated. There was much to do.

Carla sat down at her desk, pulled the typewriter to her, and began to compose a letter of confirmation. When the message was finished, folded into an envelope, and addressed to the Duncans, Carla got up from her desk and smiled. Another adventure lay before her.

CHAPTER 22

On the way home, Carla tried to keep her mind on driving, but her mind was filled with her new assignment. There was a lot of traffic. She had opened the window on the driver's side. The air was crisp; fall was quickly turning into winter. She loved this time of year in Tucson. She would have to go to New Mexico soon, and would not be here for Christmas with Marge, Anna, and Pearl. She had bought a computer game for Billy. She would leave it with Marge to give to Billy.

As she neared Saguaro Square, Carla turned off Prince onto the lane leading to her townhouse. One, two, three speed bumps and she was home. She parked the car in the carport and went to her front door, inserted the key in the lock, pushed open the door and went inside. Carla was home. Yes, this little townhouse was home. She loved every inch of it. It would be too small for a family, but for one person it was ideal; big enough to keep from feeling caged and small enough for one person to maintain.

I'll likely be gone for a few weeks, she thought. But first, I'd better call Marge.

Carla went to the kitchen counter, sat down, and pulled the phone toward her. She dialed in Marge's number. When Marge answered, she said, "Marge, you need to know that I'm going away for a little while."

"Oh?" Marge asked. "What's up?"

"I've got a new job in New Mexico to authentically decorate another old adobe house. I'll probably stay in

Taos, but I'll let you know for sure. May I leave my house keys with you?"

"Sure. How long will you be gone?"

"I don't know, maybe as much as a month. Would you look after my house?"

"Of course, I'll do whatever I can to keep an eye on things."

"Thanks, Marge."

"This job sounds interesting, but what about your business here?"

"Oh, I can check messages while I'm gone. That's no problem. And I won't be so far away that I can't come back to Tucson and handle things if I need to," Carla said.

"Sounds like you're going to miss having Christmas here," Marge said.

"I know. I'm sorry about that. I have a gift for Billy that I'll leave with you, if that's okay?" Carla asked.

"Sure, no problem, I'll tell him it's from you. Where will you be working?"

"It's a little place, off the main road between Santa Fe and Taos."

"By the way, what are you going to wear tonight?" Marge asked.

"Wear? What about tonight?"

"We're going out. Don't you remember?"

"Oh!" Carla said. "This new assignment completely wiped it out of my mind." She suddenly remembered that Marge, Pearl, Anna, and she were going to the opera, Cinderella, tonight at the theater at Arizona University. She hadn't been to many operas, but she loved them. She could imagine herself on stage, facing the lights with the audience just beyond. "I'll have to hurry, Marge. I've got to grab a bite to eat, shower, and dress."

"I'll come over at seven. Okay?" Marge asked.

"I'll be ready. I'll meet you in the carport."

Carla went to the kitchen, took a TV dinner from the freezer, and put it into the microwave. She sliced a tomato, found a container of mixed fruits, and set them on the counter. When the TV dinner was ready, she pulled a stool over to the counter and began to eat the corned beef hash. The tomato was ripe and delicious. The mixed fruits were a refreshing end to her quick bite to eat.

After a hot shower, Carla dressed, did her face, and combed her hair which fell almost to her shoulders in soft waves. Her makeup went on without any mishaps tonight. She looked at herself in the mirror as she applied a dab of cologne behind her ears.

She pulled on her undergarments and chose a dress from the closet. The dress she selected was floor length, made of gold-colored silk with a low neckline and long sleeves. She slipped the dress over her head and smoothed into it in place. She found her high-heeled gold sandals and put them on. A gold chain with an amethyst pendant completed her outfit. Carla brushed her hair again, then draped a brown shawl around her shoulders, and picked up her gold purse. She was ready for the opera!

Marge had just arrived at the carport when Carla got there. Marge was wearing black silk pants and top with a brightly colored silk sash made of patchwork.

"I'll bet you made the sash," Carla said.

"Yes," Marge said, grinning. "Do you like it?"

"It's beautiful," Carla said. "I wish I had one like it. Do you sell them?"

"I'm going to add them to my list," Marge said. "It's a good way to use up scraps from all the quilts."

"Lucky you. I can't do that. My redecorating stuff always has to be in matching sets. Why does everybody want things to match?"

"I'll miss you at Christmas," Marge said as she and Carla got into the car.

"I know. I'll probably spend Christmas Day in Taos this year," Carla said as she started the car and backed out of the driveway into the narrow street.

"Tell me all you know about your new job," Marge said as they drove out into Prince, heading toward Broadway.

"As you know, I have a job redecorating an old adobe house in a small town near Taos," Carla replied.

"Yes, you told me that. Did Jeffrey Langley get it for you?"

"No, he didn't. I got it on my own. The people were at the restoration opening downtown. You know; the old Ramirez House? What makes you think that I need Jeffrey Langley to get jobs for me?"

"I didn't mean anything by it," Marge said. "I just wondered."

"This couple saw the decorating I did for the restoration job. They just bought an old house in New Mexico and want me to redo the interior. They were impressed with my redecorating here." Carla drove carefully through the evening traffic.

"And they should be impressed. I'll miss you. A threesome isn't as much fun as a foursome," Marge said. "You're always the one that makes us do fun things."

"Well, I won't be gone forever. Besides, I'll have to come back home once in a while to attend to things at the office and check on my house," Carla said.

"Oh, I'll keep an eye on things for you. You won't have to worry," Marge said.

"Thanks, Marge, I appreciate that."

They were approaching the University. Carla turned into the entrance that led to the concert hall. There were a lot of cars already in the parking lot. She found a spot and squeezed into it. She and Marge got out and walked to the auditorium.

The performance was delightful, just as they knew it would be from the reviews in the paper. The roles were played and sung by UA music majors. They did a wonderful job and brought the well known Cinderella story to life for all who jammed the auditorium. When the opera was over, Marge and Carla left the auditorium and walked to the parking lot to retrieve the Honda and start home. Carla maneuvered the car through the traffic in the University area and got back to Broadway.

When they arrived at Carla's townhouse, she parked in the carport and the two women got out.

"Thanks for the lift," Marge said. "I really enjoyed the play tonight. It's always so much fun to do things and go places with you, Carla. You know how to have a good time. I'm going to miss you."

"You act like I'll be gone forever, Marge. It's only for a short time. I'll get the job started and be popping back and forth during the time it takes to finish it. The restoration of the house has to be done before I can even start decorating."

"Still, I'll miss you."

CHAPTER 23

The weather in early December in Tucson was not much different than November had been. The daylight was shorter and it was darker when Carla awoke in the morning. Evening also came a bit earlier now, but the weather was still mild. Once in a while, a warm jacket replaced her usual sweater.

There was much to be done at the office before she began her journey to New Mexico. The situation at her townhouse was the same. She would have to put a hold on her newspaper and mail delivery, install a timer on a living room lamp for security, and make sure bills due by the end of December were paid before she left for what might be several weeks in New Mexico.

The Monday after the opera, Carla had decided to start with the office and got out of bed at six o'clock, showered, dressed in jeans, sweater, and moccasins, preparing to go to her Design for You office. She locked her front door and got into her Honda. The weather was cool and crisp today. As she left Saguaro Square, turning onto to Prince, her attention went to the fluffy white clouds that dotted the blue sky. She had never noticed how close they seemed until she moved to southern Arizona. The mountains stood out like sentinels surrounding the city. The sun was peaking up over the mountains to the east ready to report for duty.

Carla drove to a fast-food restaurant and parked in the crowded parking lot. She went inside and ordered scrambled eggs and toast, orange juice, and coffee. As she ate her breakfast, she thought of the work that lay before her.

After breakfast, Carla continued on to Fort Lowell Road, driving along in the heavy work day morning traffic. When she reached Design for You, she parked and went inside. Her desk needed to be cleared. There were stacks of magazines, piles of brochures and the bills to be paid. I have enough work here to last me a week, Carla thought. Thank goodness I have a week to get it done! Except that doesn't take into account what comes in new.

Her busy day was spent clearing her desk and responding to her messages and mail. She also received several phone calls. One was from Mrs. Duncan, saying she was looking forward to receiving Carla's acceptance of the decorating job after she reviewed the old adobe house in San Isidro.

At lunchtime, Carla searched her food supplies. The cabinet was almost bare. She found the remaining half-empty box of crackers, and a jar of cheddar cheese spread and a tiny apple in the refrigerator. There was one bottle of orange juice left. She took the crackers, cheese spread and apple to her desk, opened a drawer, and assumed her favorite lunching position as she sat in her chair and propped her feet on the edge of the drawer. With soft music playing on the radio, she leaned back in her chair and ate her lunch.

She thought about the days ahead. What would she find in San Isidro? Would she be able to do the job she had agreed to do? Where would she stay when she was not working? Santa Fe? Taos? Or, San Isidro, itself?

Were there any inns or motels in San Isidro? What kind of weather would she encounter? Would it be colder than the weather in Tucson? Probably, the altitude was greater; she had checked on that already.

After her lunch, Carla spent the afternoon preparing to close the office for awhile. She didn't know how long she would be away, but she could handle everything remotely with her answering machine. Only her mail would stack up. At four o'clock she locked the office, went to her car, and started driving back home. As the car moved through the heavy traffic, Carla thought again about Jeffrey Langley. Where is he, and what was she going to do about him? Did he spend Thanksgiving at his house on Secret Canyon Drive? Maybe he stayed at the ranch at Texas Canyon, or maybe he spent the holiday in St. Louis. Why hadn't she heard from him? Was he spending all his time with Sydney Allen? Carla could see the tall, slender, blonde-haired woman in her mind.

Her phone was ringing as she entered her townhouse. Maybe it was Jeffrey. She hurried to it and picked it up. "Hello," she answered.

"Carla? This is Saul Watkins." Saul's voice was cheerful and low as usual. "I just wanted to check in with you. I'll be in Mexico City staying with friends for Christmas."

"Hi, Saul," Carla said. "It's good to hear from you. I'll be away for Christmas, too."

"Oh? Where are you going?"

"I'll be in either Santa Fe or Taos. I haven't made up my mind yet."

"Visiting friends?"

"No, I'm considering taking a decorating job in a place between Taos and Santa Fe. If I accept the offer, I'll probably start it in January. I thought I'd get away from here a little before then and get a feel for the general area and what I'll have to do."

"Good idea. New Mexico is interesting. Big job?"

"I suppose it is. It'll be a residence. A couple that was at the opening of the Ramirez House bought an old adobe in San Isidro. They are restoring it and want me to decorate the interior. I'll also oversee the restoration that's underway and the grounds as well."

"Sounds like fun. This will expand your field. Good for you."

"Yes, I love my little house here in Tucson, but it'll be nice to have a change for awhile."

"Well, I wanted to wish you a Merry Christmas. So, have a good holiday and good luck on this new assignment. Let me know how I can help. If I hear of any other restoration jobs, I'll give you a call."

"Thanks, Saul. Have a good time in Mexico City and Merry Christmas too."

"Thanks, 'bye."

Carla put the phone back and went to the bedroom. She took off her sweater and jeans, and put on a warm housecoat. She kicked off her moccasins and pushed her feet into a pair of soft slippers. Going to the kitchen, she took a chicken pot pie out of the freezer. She put the pie into the microwave to heat, and then found enough lettuce in the refrigerator to make a small salad. One lone tomato remained. She cut it into sections and added it to the lettuce. The last of an onion and a green pepper also went into the bowl. There was still a lot of olive oil and vinegar. She poured those over the vegetables and set the bowl at the end of the counter. She heated water and made a cup of instant coffee. When the pot pie was done, she put it next to the salad and coffee and pulled a stool up to the counter. Sitting on the high stool in her warm robe and slippers, Carla ate her dinner.

After dinner, Carla settled on the sofa, her feet tucked under her, and watched an old movie on television. It was about an old man who said he was Santa Claus and a young woman who didn't believe him. By the end, he proved that he was Santa Claus. Carla had seen the movie several times and always enjoyed it.

When the movie was over, she looked at the clock on the wall; eleven o'clock. She yawned. Getting up from the couch, she went to the bedroom, turned down the quilt, plumped her pillows, and then undressed. Stretching, she went to the bathroom and washed her face. She looked at herself in the mirror. A new adventure awaits you, she said to the Carla looking back at her. I wonder how it will turn out. Should be fun. It'll be different, any way. Yawning, she went back to the bedroom, climbed into bed, turned off the bedside lamp, and pulled the quilt up to her chin. She started to think about the future and went to sleep.

CHAPTER 24

It took three days to get ready to leave. Carla watered the plants on the patio. She checked the carport to see that everything was securely put away. She cleaned the kitchen and checked the refrigerator, clearing out leftovers and food that would be outdated. Several loads of laundry were finished in between other tasks. When everything was in order, she took a large suitcase from the closet and began to pack a week's supply of clothes; underwear, slacks and jeans, sweaters, blouses, tops. She also packed a corduroy skirt and a knit dress, two knit caps, a denim hat and her old battered cowboy hat. For footwear, she included moccasins, high-heeled brown pumps, mid-heeled black pumps, and a pair of boots for the colder weather, as well as a lined raincoat and a plaid car coat.

On Monday morning, a week before Christmas, Carla awoke and looking at the clock, slowly got out of bed. She straightened the sheets and quilt; then shook the pillows and put them back on the bed. She decided to leave the window blinds closed. She turned on the radio in the living room and listened to the weather report. Clear and cold as far east as Deming, New Mexico. Turning north at Deming, scattered rainy weather was turning to ice and snow, freezing tonight as far north as Santa Fe. After about 375 miles, Carla planned to stay over the first night in Socorro at a motel in that small city.

Standing under the hot water in the shower, she

tried to think through her list of things that needed to be done before she left for New Mexico. When she had finished showering, she picked up a fluffy towel and began to dry herself. Thoughts of Jeffrey came into her mind. Would she ever hear from him? Where was he? She would have liked to let him know where she was going. Of course, if he called and left a message, she would get it later. Still, she would have liked to hear his voice. She tried not to think of Jeffrey with Sydney Allen. If she never saw that woman again, it would be too soon.

Carla dressed in tan corduroy slacks and a brown sweater for her trip. She pulled on warm socks and boots and returned to the bathroom. After brushing her hair and applying makeup, she went back to the bedroom and put on a rust-colored knit cap, her jacket, and picked up the matching tote bag and her purse. Last night she had put her travel bags in the living room, near the door.

I might as well have breakfast in Benson, she said to herself as she walked to the front door. She looked at the clock on the living room wall; seven o'clock. She would be in the middle of morning traffic, but at least her outbound travel would be against the much heavier inbound.

She picked up her travel bags, opened the door, walked out onto the top step, and locked the door behind her with her key. She went to the carport and opened the trunk of her faithful car, putting her bags inside. Then she walked around to the driver's side, unlocked the door, and got in. The car felt cold. She started the engine and let it idle before turning on the heater. Soon warm air filled the car. She backed out of her carport and headed toward Prince Road, glancing for a moment in the rearview mirror.

"Goodbye for a while, little townhouse," she thought to herself.

The traffic was moderate as she drove through Tucson and headed east on I-10, and within forty-five minutes, she passed by the turnoff to the small town of Vail and began the climb to Benson. She would have liked to enjoy the scenery along the way, but she had to keep her eye on the road.

The traffic was moderate with trucks traveling in both directions. A group of horse trailers passed her on their way west. There were motorhomes of all sizes and descriptions. People were escaping the hard winter in the north and east, heading toward warmer Arizona climates, some continuing on to California.

When Carla reached the Ocotillo turnoff at Benson, she turned right and went to a fast food restaurant nearby. The place was nearly empty as the early breakfast crowd had already left. Three old men were sitting at a table drinking coffee. They looked up and smiled at her as she passed them. Carla found a table by the large window that faced the street. She took off her jacket and put it over the back of a chair. As she was sitting down, a young woman dressed in slacks and a tee shirt with the logo of the restaurant, The Hideout, across the front approached her table.

"Are you ready to order, or do you need a few minutes?" she asked.

"Yes, I can order now," Carla said. She picked up the menu and looked at it. "I'll have scrambled eggs, bacon, English muffin well toasted, orange juice, and coffee."

"Thanks," the waitress said, smiling. In a few minutes she was back with a mug of steaming coffee and orange juice. "Traveling?" she said.

"Yes," Carla said.

"Thought so—I didn't recognize you." She smiled and walked away, in the direction of the kitchen.

Carla looked around the restaurant. All the tables were empty except for hers and the one where the old men sat talking. Carla thought of the long drive ahead of her today. She picked up her handbag and pulled out a map of New Mexico. It was folded so that she could see I-10 and the route she would be following when she reached Deming. She sipped the orange juice as she studied the map. While she was contemplating the journey ahead, the waitress returned with Carla's order. A plate was heaped with scrambled eggs, four strips of bacon and two well toasted English muffins.

"Will there be anything else?" the young woman asked.

"No, this will be fine."

"Please enjoy your breakfast." She went away and returned just as Carla had finished buttering the muffins. The waitress refilled the coffee mug with fresh, hot coffee. She put the check on the table and left. Carla ate her breakfast slowly, enjoying every bite. Just as she finished the eggs and bacon, and had settled down to enjoy her coffee with the last of the English muffins, the old men got up from their table and prepared to leave. As they passed her table, they nodded, said "Good morning," and left after paying.

Carla was sipping the last of her coffee when a middle-aged couple came in and sat down. The woman was wearing jeans and an old sweat shirt. A man's cap was on her head. They smiled at her and sat at the other end of the room. Another couple came in and joined them. This woman was also wearing old jeans. She wore a tan canvas jacket with a real estate logo on the back and a scarf was tied around her neck.

Carla stood up to put on her jacket, left a tip on the table, and smiled at the foursome. With her handbag under her arm and the check in her hand, she walked to the counter. The waitress came from the kitchen and took the money, and smiling, said, "Have a good trip."

"Thanks," Carla said and walked out of the restaurant.

As she turned onto the ramp for I-10, Carla looked out at Benson on her right, thinking it seems like an interesting town. Probably a friendly town where everyone speaks to each other when they meet. That's the kind of place where I would really like to live. But I wouldn't make much money in the interior decorating field if I lived here. I'd have to have a different career or second job.

Just beyond Benson, the highway began to climb

again.   Texas Canyon lay ahead.   As she began the ascent to the summit of Texas Canyon, her heart began to beat harder. The pit of her stomach began to tighten. Carla was now passing the exit that led to Jeffrey's ranch. It would be so easy to make a hairpin turn and drive down the Dragoon road to the narrow lane that lead to Jeffrey's Rocking-L ranch.   Carla convinced herself to stay focused on the highway ahead.

She continued on to Wilcox, Bowie, and then San Simon. Soon after she crossed the San Simon River, she entered New Mexico. Steins lay on the left. Steins was the well-preserved remains of a railroad town that had been a repair station in the early days of railroading when New Mexico and Arizona were still territories.

Carla passed Lordsburg, also a prior railroad town. It too had been important in the early days of settling the territory.   By noon she was at the off ramp to Deming. She drove into Deming and had lunch at a MacDonald's.   After Carla had eaten her hamburger, drank her coffee, and topped off her lunch with a baked apple pie, she drove down several of the residential streets.   The old frame houses were well maintained. Most gardens were still blooming with fall flowers that survived the early morning frosts.   The yards were immaculate. Many of the houses had a wooden fence across the front of the property.

After her brief tour of Deming, she filled her tank at a gas station near the highway. Pulling away, Carla found the turnoff for state Highway 26, a shortcut to Hatch, NM.   This would take miles off the trip to Socorro, her destination for the night.   There were clusters of dwellings from time to time. As she drew closer to Hatch, the farms became more numerous. This was the heart of the red pepper industry. At this time of year, the harvests were long finished and the fields lay fallow. When Carla reached Hatch, she drove through the quaint town with many large adobe dwellings and what seemed a prosperous small business section. School was out for the Christmas holiday. The playing field beside the high school was empty.

Arriving at the intersection with Interstate 25 North, Carla turned left onto the highway and began her climb to Socorro. She passed the turnoff to Hillsboro on the left, a former hot spot in the days of mining. She passed Truth or Consequences on the right and reached the turn off to Elephant Butte which was on the south end of a large reservoir made by damming the Rio Grande River.

An hour later, as Carla was nearing the turnoff to San Antonio on the shores of the Rio Grande, she couldn't resist the temptation to drive into the tiny town. It was just a short distance from the highway, and she needed a break. She had been to San Antonio, Texas, but didn't know there was a San Antonio in New Mexico. The tour of the town didn't take long. The highpoint of San Antonio was the Raven Café and Bar. Carla went into the café and had a cup of coffee. As she sat at a table, looking at the many paintings and figurines of ravens, she was able to relax. After she had finished her coffee, she went over to the bar and ran her fingers over the old, polished wood. The magnificent wood of an antique pool table in the rear caught her attention. Even though it was not dinnertime and too early for a drink, there were people in the bar. Several of the tables were occupied. Carla stayed for forty-five minutes, then went out to her car and drove back to the highway.

Carla soon reached her destination at the Blue Dove Motel in Socorro. The Blue Dove had once been part of a large motel chain, but it was now privately owned. The owner had preserved the early motel look. The grounds were beautifully landscaped and carefully tended. The trees surrounding it had matured, although most were now without leaves. The flowers had long since gone to sleep for the winter and there were patches of snow in the shrubbery. Winter had come to this part of New Mexico.

Carla shivered as she got out of the car in front of the motel office. It was only five-thirty, but already it felt cold and the sun was beginning to set.

CHAPTER 25

Carla grabbed her bags from the trunk of her car and entered the motel office, going straight to the counter to register. She rang the bell and soon an older man came from in back.

"Good afternoon," he said, rubbing his hands together. He was of medium height, dressed in slacks and shirt with a tie. "Do you have a reservation?"

"Yes, the name is Meade," Carla said.

He pushed a registration form toward her. She took a pen and began to fill in the blank spaces.

"You have a choice of first floor or second?" he asked.

"Second floor, please." Carla thought it would be quieter on the second floor, and she might even have a better view of the mountains.

"Second floor is in this building. Dinner is served in our restaurant until nine o'clock. There are also several good restaurants in town. Let me give you a list of them." He turned and picked up a printed sheet of paper. "Here it is," he said as he handed the paper to Carla.

"Thank you."

"Enjoy your stay."

Carla smiled, turned and left the lobby and climbed the stairs to the second floor. She hoped her room on the second floor overlooked the mountains beyond the parking lot. Although the motel was situated on the highway, the units were far enough away to ensure a quiet night's rest. Carla unlocked the door of her room and stepped inside. She went to the window near the door and looked out. Yes, the mountains stood silent and tall in the distance. She turned and looked around the room. It contained a double bed, two night tables, a low chest of drawers, an easy chair, and a small table with two chairs. Although decorated in "regulation motel," it was an attractive room.

She put her bags on top of the bed and sat on the edge. It was good to be settled in for the night. The drive from Tucson had been pleasant, but she was exhausted. I'll eat dinner here at the motel, she decided. I'm too tired to go out looking for another restaurant.

She lay back on the bed and stretched. She had no intention of doing so, but Carla fell asleep. It was dark in the room when she awoke. For a moment she couldn't remember where she was. Oh, yes, she thought. I'm in Socorro. I wonder what time it is. She turned on the lamp at the side of the bed. Seven o'clock. I'd better go to the restaurant before they close.

Carla got up, stretching and yawning. She went to the small bathroom and washed her face. She debated about putting on fresh lipstick, then decided to do it. Gives a good impression, she thought, but who am I trying to impress?

After a pleasant dinner in the motel restaurant, Carla returned to her room. She closed the blinds at the window, took off her shoes, stretched out in the chair, and turned on the television. She watched the evening news and a sitcom, then, yawning, went to the bathroom where she undressed and washed her face.

Within fifteen minutes she was in her cozy nightgown and stretched out on the comfortable bed, the warm coverlet over her. Soon Carla was asleep.

When Carla opened her eyes, the room was dark. She stretched, got out of bed, and opened the blinds at the window. The bright late morning sun poured in. The mountains in the distance were illuminated with halos of light.

Carla stretched her arms over her head again, yawning. It's time to get moving, she thought. She wanted to be in Santa Fe by early afternoon, even though it was only a two hour drive. After a hot shower, Carla pulled on fresh panties, the bra she had worn yesterday, and the same jeans with a bright yellow sweater. She pulled on clean socks and pushed her feet into her moccasins. Her hair was curlier than usual. Must be the change in weather, she thought as she dragged the comb through the unruly curls. Just lipstick and cologne, she said to herself as she splashed on her favorite and colored her lips.

When she had repacked the things she had taken from her overnight bag, Carla put on her canvas jacket, picked up her handbag, and the tote bag along with a suitcase she had not opened. She left the room, pulling the door shut behind her.

After she checked her door key and picked up her receipt at the desk in the lobby, she took her bags to her car. The crisp air had made her feel hungry. She went back to the restaurant and ate a full breakfast of orange juice, poached egg, bacon, toast, and coffee.

Getting into her car after breakfast, Carla drove out into the street in front of the motel. After filling with gas, she soon was back on Highway 25, heading north toward Albuquerque. It was up grade all the way with the Rio Grande never far away. She took the bypass around the city, not taking time to sightsee. That she would do at another time. Albuquerque and its surrounding suburbs would take a few days to thoroughly explore. On the outskirts of Albuquerque, she stopped at a small café and ate a lunch of beef stew, salad, and coffee. Carla ate leisurely, looking at the surrounding landscape and enjoying the magnificent view of the mountains.

The relaxing drive from Socorro to Santa Fe only took a couple hours, but she noticed the vegetation changing with increasing altitude. She could now see glistening snow on the mountain tops in the distance. In most places it would stay until spring. Carla felt peace and tranquility just looking at the view ahead of her. That was what she liked about Tucson. The mountains, never far away, also offered the contentment she was feeling now.

She reached the outskirts of Santa Fe and began the drive toward the center of town. On either side of the street she could see glimpses of old Santa Fe mixed with the new. It was very quaint and picturesque. Arriving at the center of town, she looked for a small hotel that she had seen advertised. It was not hard to find. There it was nestled between two commercial buildings. She found a parking lot, parked her car, got out, and walked back to the hotel. The building was old and had recently been remodeled.

Carla walked in through the tall wooden doors. There was a small lobby with the registration desk along the back wall. "May I help you?" asked a young woman standing behind the desk.

"Yes, I would like a room for the night."

"We have a single on the second floor, near the back. We are just about full up."

"Nothing along the front?" Carla asked.

"No, I'm sorry. We just have that one room left."

"I'll take it, then."

"For how many nights?" the young woman asked.

"Just one," Carla replied. She filled out the registration form and was given a key. Carla went back to the parking lot and got her bags out of the Honda. Returning to the hotel, she looked in the shop windows along the narrow street. Posters, porcelain, paintings, and leather work were displayed in the shop windows. Carla felt exhilarated, and not just from the higher altitude. Santa Fe gave her a lift. She would have liked to share this with someone, and she wondered if Jeffrey had ever been in Santa Fe.

I really don't know much about Jeffrey, she thought as she reached the hotel. She entered the small elevator in the lobby and went to the second floor. It didn't take long to walk down the hall to the room she had been assigned. There was a window at the end of the hall. She went to it and looked out. Another narrow street stretched out in either direction. Across from her was a row of small shops.

The small room contained a double bed with a night table beside it, a long low dresser, a very small table, and an upholstered arm chair. The bathroom was very utilitarian with a sink, a shower, and a toilet. A tiny window above the toilet let in light and a view of a mountain in the distance.

Carla could hear that someone was showering in the room next door. The sound came through as though they were in her bathroom. Nice to have neighbors close by, Carla laughed to herself.

She decided to put her bags in the corner beside the table. The small closet was too narrow. After putting away the bags, she decided to walk around the neighborhood of the hotel. She went down to the lobby in the small elevator. The same clerk was standing behind the desk. She waved to Carla, and Carla waved back. Out on the sidewalk, Carla was glad she was wearing her jacket. The air was very chilly.

She turned to the right and walked to the end of the block. The Santa Fe River at this time of the year was a narrow stream that divided the area. Beyond her was a large building that looked like a school. On this side of the stream was a narrow street with shops on just one side.

She crossed the street and walked slowly past the shops. Midway down the block, she came to a restaurant. She pushed open the door and went inside. She had expected to be the only customer as it was still early. However, there were two people sitting at a table near the window eating dinner.

Carla found a table and sat down. As she was picking up the menu, a young man arrived with water. "Good afternoon," he said. "May I bring you coffee? Or tea?"

Carla picked up the menu. "Coffee, please." She smiled at him.

"Yes, ma'am. If you have any questions about the menu, just ask. I'll be nearby and checking on you in a few minutes."

"Thank you," Carla said. She began to read the menu.

When the waiter returned with a coffee pot in hand, he filled Carla's empty cup and asked, "Are you ready to order?"

"Yes," Carla said.

"And what can we get you?"

"I'll have the salmon and a tossed salad."

"Very good choice, the salmon is fresh. We get it flown in every week. What kind of potatoes with that?"

"The stuffed baked potato and green beans please."

"Great. We have freshly baked dinner rolls. Would you like to have some?"

"Yes, please."

"Comin' up. And the dressing for your salad?"

"French."

"Thank you."

Carla removed her jacket and put it on the chair next to her. While Carla waited for her salad, she looked around the room. Now there were several more people in the restaurant. She looked out through the large window beside the door and could see the building across the stream.   As several young people were walking around, Carla surmised it may be a boarding school.

The waiter arrived with Carla's salad and placed it in front of her. He put a plate of hot rolls and a bowl of butter on the table. She smiled up at him and he smiled back.   When he left, she poured the small dish of dressing on her salad, took a roll and buttered it, and began to eat. She hadn't realized until that first bite of salad just how hungry she was.

Carla sat back and sighed as she swallowed a bite of salad. She was becoming aware that she was tired, even though the day had not been that long.   When the entrée arrived, the aroma from the salmon made Carla's mouth water. Carla had finished eating the last bite of her leisurely meal when the waiter came back to the table.

"Here's the dessert menu."   He placed a card in front of her. "Do you need time to consider it?"

"No," Carla said, looking at the first item on the card. "I'll have the chocolate cookie pizza."

"The servings are big. Enough for two people or more," the young man said.

"Can you give me just half a serving?" Carla said.

"Sure. That's the way most people order it, but we have some customers who'll eat all of it." He laughed. "Wine or coffee to go with that?"

"Coffee, please."

When the serving of dessert pizza arrived, Carla gasped. The slice was huge. "I wonder what I would have done had I ordered the whole cookie pizza?" she said, laughing.

"It takes a hungry person to eat an entire cookie pizza," the waiter said, smiling.

Carla waded through the delicious dessert, wiping the crumbs from her chin as she chewed the last bite. She drank her coffee, picked up her handbag, and went to the cashier's desk to pay for her meal. She had added a generous tip to the bill as the waiter had given her excellent service.

When she left the restaurant, she crossed the narrow street to the bank of the stream that fronted the restaurant. The sign on the low wall that separated the stream from the sidewalk said it was a river, but it looked like a narrow creek to Carla. The area was illuminated by the street lights. It looked peaceful. Carla drank in the tranquility for a few moments, then turned and walked toward her hotel.

The room felt inviting when she opened the door. It's about as plain as it can get, and yet—. I must be tired, she said to herself. She took off her jacket, went to her travel bag, and took out her warm nightgown. Then she sat down on the edge of the bed to undress. Pulling off her moccasins and socks, she thought about the past two days.

Traveling to Santa Fe was a big step for Carla. She had made a lot of trips alone since she graduated from college and began her professional life. Why was this one different? She thought of her brief time with Peter. She had met him in college. He was a student majoring in law. He was her age, medium height, well built, dark hair, and great smile. His home was in Glen Burnie near Baltimore. She shivered thinking about him. They had clicked from the first moment they had met. Within a few months, they knew they would spend the rest of their lives together. By the time they graduated, they had made plans to marry, settle down in Baltimore where Peter had the offer of a job in a law firm. Baltimore was a good location for an interior decorator. Carla found work with a local decorating firm. Baltimore was not too far from Carla's home town, Oakland, Maryland.

Her aunt approved of Peter Meade. She had met him when she visited Carla at college. He came from a good family. The family name was well known in Maryland. This sort of thing meant a lot to Aunt Phyllis. Carla and Peter had married about a year after graduation. It was a small wedding. They settled down in a small apartment on the edge of Baltimore. Mr. and Mrs. Peter Meade.

It should have gone well. Both of them had found jobs in their chosen professions. The apartment was nice, situated in a decent neighborhood. They had made friends in the area. They were in love, or thought they were. Aha, the key word was "thought."

The good times didn't last too long. Marriage brought them too close together. They discovered things about each other that they didn't really like. Peter liked to hunt and fish. Carla liked walking through the woods, seeing an animal and watching it from a distance. She liked to see fish swimming in clear water. Carla liked to dance; Peter didn't care for dancing. Peter liked to play poker; Carla didn't care for poker. Carla wanted to have a child right away; Peter wanted to wait for a few years before becoming a father. Within a year, they knew their marriage was not going to work. They had made a mistake. Being a lawyer, Peter was able to find someone to quickly write up the divorce. What Carla had thought would be a lifetime together was "done away with" in a matter of months.

After the divorce, Carla had packed her things and left. What Peter did with the furniture was his own decision. She ultimately moved to Tucson and Peter had probably stayed in Baltimore. She didn't know and didn't care.

Carla turned to pick up her nightgown lying at the foot of the bed. She pulled it on and stood up. In the small bathroom she washed her face to remove the makeup. Then she went back to the bed and stretched out, pulling the warm blanket over her.

I'm not going to think about anything else tonight, she resolved to herself as she turned on her side. I'm just going to sleep. I'll be in Taos tomorrow and I have a reservation there. It's only three days until Christmas. I wonder what Christmas in Taos is like? Well, I'll soon find out. She yawned, turned on her side, and closed her eyes.

CHAPTER 26

After breakfast, Carla filled her car's gas tank. She had intended to follow the scenic High Road through Penasco to Taos, but the service station attendant told her that the conditions of that winding road are not good. It had snowed during the night and although there was not much accumulation in Santa Fe, the higher elevations had received a lot.

"The main highway has been cleared and traffic is moving. If it was me, I'd stick to the main road," he said.

"Thank you," Carla said. "I'll take your advice."

Carla was having no trouble on the main highway. The sky was cloudy but there was no wind and no snow. It was cold, though. Carla was glad she had brought a heavy jacket. It lay on the seat beside her. She looked out the window at the scenery as she traveled along Route 68 with a fair amount of traffic. Cars passed her going toward Santa Fe. There were cars ahead of her and behind her as she made her way to Taos.

When she reached Taos, everything was covered in white. She stayed in the tracks along the main street on her way to the plaza. Reaching Taos Plaza, she found a parking place and got out, locking the car.

She walked across the plaza to the row of buildings on the other side. The tires of the few cars passing by crunched the snow. The Inn on the Plaza was in front of her. She went over to the front entrance and pulled open the big door. The lobby was warm from a log fire in the corner fireplace. She walked over to it, took off her gloves, and warmed her hands. After standing there for a few minutes warming herself, she crossed over to the registration desk. The young woman at the desk registered Carla and gave her a key.

She pulled on her gloves, went back to her car, and took out her luggage. Returning to the hotel across the snow covered square, she looked at the building. It was old and very beautiful. She had admired the way the lobby was decorated. If the rest of the Inn on the Plaza was as beautiful, she was going to enjoy her stay very much.

Before long Carla was in her second floor room with two windows overlooking the historic plaza. She walked to the windows and pulled aside the drapes. She looked out on the snow covered square. All the way from Santa Fe the snow had softened the harsh contours of the land. Now, it rounded the edges of the old buildings that lined the historic site.

She turned from the window, letting the drapes fall back into place. She hugged herself to take away the lingering chill. The bed looked inviting. Only two days until Christmas. She would enjoy herself here and explore the town. She wanted to see the Governor Bent Museum, Kit Carson's house, and several of the other historic places, especially the historic San Francisco de Asis Church in Ranchos de Taos, built in the late 1700's. The art shops are a must. She wanted time to walk through them and look at all the displays. She hadn't sketched or painted in several years. Maybe she would buy a sketch book and capture some of the sights and views.

Carla left her room and returned to the lobby. She was going to find a nice place to eat lunch. Maybe tonight she would have dinner at the hotel. The clerk at the desk suggested she try the tiny restaurant at the far end of the plaza for lunch. "The Lantern," she said. "I eat there a lot. There should be a nice crowd of writers, artists, and musicians. You'll love it. And the food's pretty good, too."

"Thanks, I'll give it a try," Carla said.

Carla crossed the narrow street to the plaza. There was a covering of snow in the flower beds that were bordered by large rocks. The shrubs and cactuses had long since put on their winter appearances and had settled in for the cold weather.

When she reached the far end of the plaza, Carla stepped down into the street and crossed over to the sidewalk. There it was. An old barn lantern hung beside the door. Carla went inside. The place was crowded and several people were waiting for tables. A server came up to her and said, "You'll have to wait about ten minutes. Is that all right?"

"Certainly," Carla said. In less than ten minutes she was taken to a table for two. It was in a corner by the front windows. From her chair, she had a view of the plaza and the front of the hotel where she was staying.

The menu was interesting. There were a lot of dishes whose names she didn't recognize. However, she found one that was familiar to her—chili con carne. When the server returned to take her order, she said, I'll have the chili con carne and coffee, please."

While she was waiting for her lunch, Carla looked around the room. It seemed to be occupied by a mixture of business people on their lunch break, some tourists, and a sprinkling of townspeople.

I think Jeffrey would like it here, she said to herself. Now, what made her think of that? What brought Jeffrey Langley into her mind now? She had purposely decided that she would not think of him, but he had invaded her mind anyway.

Is he with Sydney, she wondered. Are they in St. Louis, lunching in some exclusive restaurant with their friends? Or maybe they have taken a Caribbean cruise for the Christmas holidays?

Carla's lunch arrived. She thanked the server and took a bite of the chili, served in a bowl with no beans. The beans were in a separate dish. There was hot, crusty bread on a little plate. Interesting, she thought. I've never had it this way before, she thought.

When Carla had finished her lunch, the server came back. "Ready for dessert? The cook made apple pies today. Want some apple pie and more coffee?"

"I'd better not," Carla said. "I've got to watch my figure."

The server smiled as she put the check on the table. "I know what you mean. Well, enjoy your visit to Taos and come back while you're in town."

"Thank you," Carla said. She paid for her lunch at the cashier's desk and went out to the sidewalk. Small groups of people were standing and talking, or walking around the plaza. Others were walking purposefully, bent on an errand. Carla crossed over to the plaza and walked to the other end.

She turned and started walking up the street, away from Taos Plaza. Old historic buildings lined both sides of the main street. There were more restaurants, shops selling various things from souvenirs and antiques to paintings, sculptures, and jewelry made by artisans in the area. Other people were doing the same thing Carla was doing, walking along the sidewalks, gazing into the shop windows. The wind was now blowing and it was cold.

Carla crossed the narrow street when the traffic thinned, and walked back toward the plaza. A bus loaded with people and skis piled on a small trailer, passed her. The passengers in the bus were obviously on their way to one of the many ski resorts in the area. Maybe I should take up skiing, Carla thought. That would be different. Living in Tucson, you'd have to travel quite a distance to ski, although, one could go to Mount Lemmon nearby. That is, when there was enough snow.

Carla returned to the hotel and went to her room. She took off her jacket and pulled the wool cap off her head. Sitting on the edge of the bed, she wriggled her feet out of her moccasins and stretched out on the bed, pulling the covers over her. I should be checking on the office, she thought. I'll do that as soon as I take a little rest. She yawned and closed her eyes.

When Carla awakened, the room was in shadows. She glanced at the bedside clock. Four o'clock. I was going to check messages at the office, she said to herself. She got out of bed, kicking the covers out of the way. She went to the little table where she reached for the phone. The next hour was spent going over incoming messages and making notes of unfinished business. She was surprised to hear a recorded message from Jeffrey, "Hi, I wanted to check in with you and wish you a Merry Christmas and a Happy New Year. Things are hectic at this end. Tucson must be looking a lot like Christmas now. Sorry I have to miss it. See you when I get back to town. Have a good Christmas and New Year."

Well, she thought; that was nice of him. He doesn't know that I'm not in Tucson. But, how would he know? And, I hope he has a nice holiday, too. Sydney will see to that, I'm sure.

When she had finished her office work, it was time for dinner. I might as well eat here at the hotel, she said to herself. After taking a shower, combing her hair, and putting on makeup, Carla dressed. She was wearing brown slacks, matching pumps and a turquoise sweater. She picked up her handbag and left the room.

The dining room in the hotel was at the end of the lobby. It was arranged with an atrium four stories high with a small flower garden in the center. Flowers and plants were in pots; the predominating plants were poinsettias for this time of year. She was given a table at the edge of the atrium. The server suggested the special of the day, Cornish game hen with vegetables. A tossed salad and clear chicken broth would precede it. Carla ordered the special as suggested.

"Would you care for a cocktail?" the server said.

"I'll have a glass of white wine," Carla said.

"I think you'd like the house wine—a pinot grigio from Napa Valley. It's very good."

When she was served, Carla sat there looking around her at the other diners as she sipped her wine. The room was filling up. Most of them are guests, she thought. But others were shedding coats and some of the women were wearing hats. A waiter came to the table carrying a tray. He placed a bowl of broth and a plate of salad in front of her. "Your entrée will be served soon," he told her. Carla sampled the broth. Ah, very tasty. When she had finished it, she poured dressing on the salad and began to eat.

The room was now filled. Carla looked around, not seeing any empty tables. Everybody was eating, talking, and laughing. It was very pleasant. Much more fun than eating alone in her house.

Her house—Carla thought of the townhouse in Tucson. She missed it. She missed her neighbor, Marge, and the other girls who made up the foursome. She missed Jeffrey.

Oh, don't think about him, she thought. He's much too busy to try to see me. Where was he tonight, two days before Christmas? What was he doing? Was he with Sydney? Carla could see Sydney in a long dress, her blonde hair swirling around her shoulders. Her makeup would be perfect; not one eyelash out of place.

The waiter arrived and brought the entrée. The game hen looked delicious. "Thank you," Carla said.

"You're welcome. I'll check back with you to see if you need anything else."

Carla ate leisurely, savoring every bite. This was the life. She envied people like Jeffrey who lived from house to house, hotel to hotel, never having to worry about cooking, cleaning, gardening. She was glad she was on an expense account.

Dessert was served promptly after Carla had finished her entrée. After she ate the last bite of chocolate ice cream and drank another cup of coffee, Carla left the restaurant dining room. It was still full. They would be busy for at least a couple of hours, she thought.

She went to the lobby and sat down on a small sofa. The room was almost full. Nearly all the chairs and sofas were occupied with people talking and laughing. Yes, she was in Taos. A thrill of excitement passed through her body. The very name of the place conjured up visions of ancient pueblos, sacred mesas, Kit Carson, the Santa Fe Trail, not to mention wintertime skiing. She had never been to Taos before. This was a wonderful opportunity to walk its streets, try to fathom its secrets, even dip into its past.

Now she would have the chance. She would be nearby working within the patched walls and sturdy foundations of an old house. Perhaps those walls would talk to her and tell her their secrets. She would learn something of the history they had witnessed. She got up, walked up the staircase, holding onto the carved banister. The day after tomorrow was Christmas. She had nothing to do, no family or friends with whom to spend the day. She would go to the little town of San Isidro. She would go there and see the house she was going to redecorate.

When Carla reached her room, she unlocked the door and went inside. As she undressed and washed her face, she wondered what San Isidro would look like now. It was a small town.

She yawned, stretched, and got into bed. As she pulled the covers over her, she yawned and found herself humming, "San Isidro, here I come," as she drifted off to sleep.

CHAPTER 27

A bright winter sun sifted through the space between the two panels of the window draperies. As its rays crossed Carla's face, she awoke and slowly everything sorted itself out.

Yes, she was in Taos, New Mexico. Today was Christmas Eve and she was going to San Isidro. She got out of bed and went to the table in the corner of the room. Turning on the lamp, she got out a map of the area. The road to San Isidro went south, more or less, for about ten or twelve miles. San Isidro was just a tiny dot. Well, she would find that dot today and see the adobe house. Maybe she would be able to see the inside and get some idea of the work that was required. Then she could call Mrs. Duncan to tell her of her initial assessment and whether or not she would take the job.

Carla went to the bathroom, stripped off her nightgown and took a hot shower. After the shower and rubbing herself dry, she put on her makeup and combed her hair. In the bedroom, she dressed in blue jeans and a pink turtleneck sweater. After pulling on her boots, she took her briefcase, picked up her handbag, and put the straps over her shoulder. She took her jacket and wool cap, and walking out of the room, locked the door behind her.

"Good morning," the young woman greeted as Carla passed the desk. Christmas carols were playing on the sound system.

"Good morning," Carla said smiling.

There were only three other people in the dining room. Carla found a table by a window and sat down. Soon a waitress arrived and took her order for breakfast: poached eggs, waffles, bacon, coffee, and orange juice.

Carla looked at the little garden in the center of the room. It reminded her of her patio in Tucson and the good times she had with her friends there. She wished for a moment that she were with them.

After breakfast, Carla went to her car and started the trip to San Isidro. The road south began with a climb to the top of a mountain, and then downhill, traveling the narrow highway. Snow was piled on both sides, the pines and spruces lining the roadway. Suddenly a village came into sight. The bluffs on the west side of the two lane highway cast long shadows into the steep ravines. She was nearing a break in the hills and an exit off the highway. She could see a scattering of flat-topped adobe buildings, the Adelita Mountains rising behind them. She exited onto a narrow street that was in need of repair as she swerved to avoid the potholes. In places, only remnants of blacktop remained. At the end of the lane was the tallest building in the village with a cross on the top of a steeple. She had arrived — San Isidro.

Suddenly Carla was startled as she recognized some of the buildings. Turning her head to see everything, she drove slowly through the village. Memories came roaring back to her, filling her mind — they were overwhelming. San Isidro — Daddy — Maria — Herself ... Emily.

The memories that she had driven out of her mind and kept hidden for so many years were returning. Daddy had been gone a long time — since the Vietnam War. She wondered if Maria was still living in San Isidro. Emily had been replaced by Carla, the person she now called herself.

She proceeded slowly, arriving at the spot where her old house had once stood, across and down the street from the church. Checking her notes, THIS was the address Mrs. Duncan had given her to redecorate. Yes, there it was, it's front looking fresh and new. But, it looked different. What was it? Oh, maybe the windows — some windows had been cut into the front wall facade. There were only a couple windows before on the front of the adobe, and there was a front door too. There had not been a door onto the street when she had lived there. One had to go in through the gate and walk to the back. Well, it's what I should have expected, she thought. I suppose the Duncans have modernized the interior as well.

She drew up in front of the long adobe building that stretched across the rutted lane from the old church with its rusty iron fence. As she got out of her car, a shaggy dog came up to her wagging his tail. She reached down to pat his head as a man came toward her.

"Welcome home, Emily. I'd know you anywhere."

She turned to him and clasped his outstretched hands. "Joe Ortega? I can't believe it's really you. Nobody has called me Emily for many years. I can't believe I'm here. How long has it been?"

"A long, long time. Do you want to see the house? Mrs. Duncan said someone would be coming." Joe Ortega, now old with white hair showing below his battered black hat, led the way to the huge double doors. "Mrs. Duncan called me and said that someone called Carla Meade was coming to San Isidro. I didn't expect to see Emily Bartlett." He walked up the two steps to the doors.

"This is the new way into the house. You'll see, things are somewhat changed around now." Carla went through the opened doors into a hallway. Joe led her through the door on the right. "This is the kitchen — all modern now."

"Hmm, nice," Carla said.

"On this side of the hall is the living room and dining room," Joe said.

They walked into the big room with windows on the front wall and a door opening onto the back porch. Joe led her through another doorway down a hall to the bedrooms. At the end was a tiny room.

"My old bedroom," Carla said. "At least, it looks the same."

"It's so little, there wasn't anything they could do to make it different. Maybe use it as a closet." He chuckled.

Carla laughed with him.

"Well, you've seen it. What do you think? Think anyone can decorate it to suit the Duncans?" Joe asked.

"Joe," said Carla. "I am Carla Meade and am now an interior decorator. It's a long story."

"I'll leave you here to walk around and look it over.

Just put the lock on when you leave. I live across the street, next door to the church. It's good to see you after all these years."

Turning to Joe, Carla said, "It was wonderful seeing you again too, Joe. Oh, Maria. How is she? Do you ever see her? Is she still living in San Isidro?"

"Maria's in the cemetery now. Been there three — maybe four years," Joe said.

"Oh." Carla put her hand over her mouth. "I'm sorry; I hadn't remembered her all these years. And now I find out that she's gone."

"Not many folks left here in San Isidro. Oh, some come back on All Saint's Day, but most of them live in other places now. Well, I'd best be going." Joe tipped his hat and left her alone in the house.

Carla walked through the house again, looking from room to room. This did not seem the house that little Emily Bartlett had lived in with daddy and Maria so many years ago. It was like a new creation, a playhouse someone had bought from a toy store and put together.

Carla left a few minutes after Joe had gone, locking the door behind her. Her decision had been made.

CHAPTER 28

Carla was standing beside her car when an old pickup drove by. When the driver passed the church, he started backing up. The pickup stopped in front of her car. A tall man got out, dressed in jeans, boots, and a battered leather jacket. An old felt western-styled hat topped his graying hair.

Astonished, Carla looked at him. *"Jeffrey?"* she questioned.

The man looked at her standing in front of the old adobe house. He blinked his eyes and looked again. *"Emily?"*

"My name is Carla." She swallowed.

"You're little Emily—I don't believe it," he said as he moved over to her. "But ... it is you. I *knew* there was something. Every time I looked at you, I had a funny feeling that wouldn't go away. I kept thinking, 'I know this girl,' ... but from where?" Now he was at her side, his arms around her. "What are you doing here in San Isidro? Why aren't you in Tucson?"

"What are you doing here?" Carla asked. "Why aren't you in St. Louis?"

Jeffrey pushed her away, gazed at her for a moment, then pulled her toward him again. "I was going back tomorrow. I've been at my ranch near here for a few days taking care of end of the year business. I just came into town to get a few supplies at the general store. But tell me, what brought you to San Isidro?"

"Some people—Mr. and Mrs. Duncan—bought our

254

old house. They renovated it and are making a lot of changes." She pointed to the front door and windows of the old adobe.

"Yeah, I can see that," Jeffrey said.

"They heard about me at the restoration project in Tucson and got in touch with me. They want me to decorate the interior." She waved her hand toward the house. "I came here to look at it and decide if I want to do the job." She swallowed and looked down at her feet, then looked back at the house. "I don't think I want the job. I—I," she stammered, "I couldn't work on a house that had been —."

"Had been Doc's and yours?" Jeffrey reached out and touched her shoulder. "I can understand that. So, what will you do?"

"I thought I'd call them and tell them I can't take the job."

"Will you tell them why?"

Carla shook her head.

"You have to tell them something. They'll want to know the reason."

"I—I guess you're right. Oh, this is all too much." Carla started to cry, and then wiped her eyes with her gloved hand.

"Why did you stop here, in front of my old house? That is … Emily's old house?" she asked.

"I was just checking something on the truck. Heard an engine rattle I hadn't heard before. Lucky I did, otherwise I'd have missed you. You and I have a lot of talking to do, young lady. Why this 'Carla' business?" Jeffrey paused and then said, "Let's walk down to the café and get some hot coffee. We can talk better there out of the cold."

It was a short walk to San Isidro's small business section. Carla followed Jeffrey into the little café. She didn't remember it being here. But there were a lot of things that she had carefully stored away, never intending to open the mental file cabinet again.

When they entered the café, the warmth surrounded Carla like friendly arms. She unbuttoned her coat and let it slip off her shoulders. Jeffrey went to a small table near the window and pulled out a chair for her. She took off her jacket and put it over the back of the chair, then sat down. She looked around her. There were several people in the café, mostly men. They looked at her briefly, and then went back to what they were doing.

Jeffrey sat in the chair across from Carla and said, "Remember this place?"

Carla shook her head. "I don't think it was here."

"Yep, it was. But it was a whiskey joint. I came here once in a while with my dad, but it was off limits to women and girls. It was turned into a café when the original owner died. His daughter and her husband took it over. By that time there were two other bars in town."

"Do you come here often? To San Isidro, I mean?" Carla said.

"Twice a year. I check out the ranch, spend a few days hunting and hiking around the W-Lazy-L, then back to St. Louis, or Tucson, or wherever I have to be next."

A middle-aged woman, an apron tied around the waist of her long-sleeved dress, took their orders for coffee. When she had gone away, Jeffrey asked, "Are you staying in Taos?"

"Yes," Carla said, "at the Plaza Inn."

"Nice place, I've stayed there a few times. How long will you be here? I mean, in this area?"

"I'll go back to Tucson the day after Christmas."

"That's the day after tomorrow."

"Yes, I know." The coffee arrived and Carla thanked the woman and smiled at her. As soon as she and Jeffrey were alone, she said, "I feel so strange being here again. I'm trying to adjust to my feelings."

"What I can't figure out is why you're not Emily now. Why are you called Carla?" Jeffrey asked.

"When Daddy was drafted for Vietnam, he took me to Maryland to live with Aunt Phyllis. My grandmother, who Aunt Phyllis also cared for, was also named Emily. Aunt Phyllis started calling me Carla, which is my middle name, to tell us apart."

"Where is your father now?" Jeffrey asked.

"He was killed in Vietnam." Carla took a sip of coffee, trying to organize her thoughts as Jeffrey's comments triggered more memories. "W-Lazy-L?" she asked ... "Isn't that the ranch just north of town, across the river?

"Yes," Jeffrey replied. "That's where you and I used to go riding, remember?"

"*Jeffrey,*" Carla gasped as she clasped his hands. "*You're Gary Langford?*" Her eyes blinked rapidly as this new realization began to sink in. Carla sat dazed as she stared across the table at the man she thought she had first met only months ago. The cowboy, who sat with her in the bathtub helping decide where to put the brass heron, was the Gary she knew as a child.

"I can't believe this!" Carla exclaimed as she studied Jeffrey's face closely. Touching his cheek with her fingers she said, "I knew you as Gary Langford — why are you called Jeffrey Langley now?" her eyes riveted on his.

"Same sort of thing happened to me as it did to you," Jeffrey said. "Jeffrey Garrison Langford. Isn't that a mouthful?" He laughed. "My Dad always called me Gary." Carla waited for him to continue.

"As you know, my Aunt Doris looked after me when Dad died in the river. We lived here on the ranch until I was old enough to start high school. For a number of reasons, Aunt Doris thought it best to move back to St. Louis. We were closer to family and I could go to a better high school. What happened was that Aunt Doris married Dexter Langley, a successful business man from St. Louis. Dex had made a fortune in the oil business, but had never previously married." Jeffrey paused, thinking back, "He and I got along great. We became really close and did everything together like my Dad and I used to do. When Uncle Dexter was diagnosed with cancer, he asked if I would consent to being adopted so that the Langley name would carry on. I agreed. The name Langley was not much different than Langford, and he had become closer to me than my real father. From then on, my name has been Jeffrey Langley."

Carla was nodding as she began to understand.

"When you've finished your coffee," Jeffrey said, "let's go up to the ranch. We'll talk and fill in more of the blanks for each other. Hey, why don't you spend Christmas with me at the ranch? The folks there would love it. They don't get much company."

"I—I don't know if that's a good idea."

"Oh, come on. It's better than being in a hotel full of tourists."

"Well —."

"You can follow me back to the ranch. Won't take long. Come on, drink your coffee, and let's go."

Carla didn't remember the narrow road that she was driving. They had left San Isidro, Jeffrey in front of her in his pickup and she following behind in her car. There was snow piled on either side of the cleared gravel road. She glanced at the mountains ahead of her. Taos was on the other side. So many discoveries in the last hour had left her thoughts spinning. Maybe I should reconsider redecorating the Duncan's house, Carla thought as her eyes marveled at the beauty of the scenery that lay ahead. Her feelings toward Jeffrey were becoming warmer as she now understood that he was a missing link to her past.

As they neared the river now almost iced over, Carla began to feel afraid. Suddenly a picture came to her mind. A summer day, the water high in the river as it tumbled along. As vividly as if it were yesterday, she could see a man, Gary's father, struggling in the raging water. Carla screamed, "Oh, no!" and she was little Emily for a moment. Then her mind quickly returned to the present and she continued across the bridge that now spanned the ice-filled river.

Boyhood Ranch near San Isidro, NM

In a short time they arrived at the ranch house. It looked the same as it had when Carla was that little girl called Emily. Jeffrey parked his truck near the porch. Carla pulled her car in beside his, got out, and walked to the porch with him.

"Is your Aunt Doris still alive?" Carla asked.

"Aunt Doris died several years ago," Jeffrey replied. "My ranch foreman and his family have been living here. They keep a room ready for me in the old bunkhouse, but the ranch house is theirs."

Jeffrey was opening the front door.

"I don't know how, but suddenly things are coming back to me that I haven't thought about in years." After a brief scan of the room, Carla said, "The house looks the same. Nothing's changed."

"Oh, a few things are different. Stuff wore out and got replaced. But it's pretty much the same as it was," Jeffrey said as his eyes surveyed the room with hers.

Carla sat down in a rocking chair. Jeffrey knelt on one knee beside her. "When you told me you had been married to a guy named Peter Meade, I didn't even think to ask what your maiden name was," he said. "I might have put it all together then."

Carla looked at Jeffrey and in a quiet voice replied, "I kept his name because it had become my professional name. I was already an interior decorator."

"Wow! This is so hard to believe; so much has happened." Jeffrey said.

Carla replied, "And now we're back to where we were many years ago."

"I love you, Carla," Jeffrey's voice whispered.

"I love you too," she said.

Jeffrey stood up, pulled Carla out of the rocking chair, and put his arms around her.

Carla could hear voices in the back of the house. She looked into Jeffrey's eyes. "What about Sydney?" she asked softly.

"Sydney is just a friend. She has never meant anything more to me. She's a mixed up, spoiled woman with too much money, too much imagination, and too insensitive to what others think. I don't love her, I never have, and I don't think she could ever really love me, or anyone else for that matter. As long as she has a big bank account, Sydney will be happy."

Looking down at her eyes he said, "But I'll be happy with just you, my little Emily Carla Bartlett Meade."

"Are you sure, Mr. Gary Jeffrey Langford Langley?" Carla giggled.

"I was never surer of anything in my life." Jeffrey pulled her close and gently kissed her.